"Each piece, not more than 300 words, not more than a page of illustrations. Surely that was daunting and exciting for writers and artists. And they did it! Very, very, very well. This collection is fascinating, exhilarating! Each word, each line precise and precious. The reader gasps, sighs, laughs, cries, longs, hopes. And relishes the lines and words again and again."

Rofel G Brion
*writer of poetry and short prose; writing coac*h

"*Missed Connections* is a garden of manifold small flowers. Its forms of austere beauty explode, and you are invited to squint. There are worlds within worlds here, each existing for no more than a minute of your time. Oh reader, beware the rabbit holes!"

Gwee Li Sui
poet, graphic artist, literary critic

"In brief, sparkling stories, this anthology forms a compelling archipelago of life. A wonderful compilation of important voices, ready to keep you company."

Laurel Flores Fantauzzo
author, My Heart Underwater

"What does a story need to bring you on a journey? Length is not an issue, and the works in *Missed Connections* illustrate just that. Fine flash always surprises you even if you know where it's going, and the works in this collection unravelled like puzzle pieces, seeing you through to the reward of the ending."

Shamini Aphrodite
fiction editor, Suspect literary journal

T0274417

missed connections

missed connections
microfiction from Asia

editors
felix cheong
noelle q. de jesus

Marshall Cavendish
Editions

Published in 2023 by Marshall Cavendish Editions
An imprint of Marshall Cavendish International

Other Marshall Cavendish Offices:
Marshall Cavendish Corporation, 800 Westchester Ave, Suite N-641,
Rye Brook, NY 10573, USA • Marshall Cavendish International (Thailand)
Co Ltd, 253 Asoke, 16th Floor, Sukhumvit 21 Road, Klongtoey Nua, Wattana,
Bangkok 10110, Thailand • Marshall Cavendish (Malaysia) Sdn Bhd, Times
Subang, Lot 46, Subang Hi-Tech Industrial Park, Batu Tiga, 40000 Shah
Alam, Selangor Darul Ehsan, Malaysia

Marshall Cavendish is a registered trademark of Times Publishing Limited

National Library Board, Singapore Cataloguing in Publication Data

Name(s): Cheong, Felix , editor. | De Jesus, Noelle Q., editor.
Title: Missed connections : microfiction from Asia / editors, Felix Cheong,
Noelle Q. de Jesus.
Other Title(s): Microfiction from Asia
Description: Singapore : Marshall Cavendish Editions, 2023.
Identifier(s): ISBN 978-981-5113-32-7 (paperback)
Subject(s): LCSH: Short stories, Singaporean (English) | Short stories,
English--Asia.
Classification: DDC 828.99503--dc23

Printed in Singapore

"Only connect..."
EM Forster

Contents

Preface   17
Noelle Q. de Jesus

Resurrection   19
Jose Y. Dalisay

Parenthood   21
Diana Mandac

The Painting   22
Vicky Chong

Curry Puffs   24
Paul GnanaSelvam

Birdsong   26
Chen Cuifen

What I Learned from Mum   27
Dora Tan

Showbusiness   28
Charina Mercado

I'm Coming to Help You   30
Wesley Leon Aroozoo

Crossing The Rice Field   31
Shinnen Cahandig

The Cynical Sisters   32
Rachel Tey

White Jade, White Elephant   34
Claire A. Miranda

The People on My Boat   36
Reanne Mak

Huawei Rescue   37
Maya Calica Collins

New Year's Resolution   38
Suraya Md Nasir

Inheritance 39
Cherrie Sing

Each Other 40
Yvette Fernandez

A Feast For Neneng 42
Nixie E. Serna

We Played with Same Dolls but Invented Our Own Games 44
Anisha Ralhan

Found Wanting 46
Abigail C. James

Love Child 48
Gem Deveras Mañosa

Home and My Lot 50
Libay Linsangan Cantor

Those Left Behind 52
Gene Tamesis, Jr.

Curating Life and Death 54
Dengcoy Miel

Sweet Release 55
Risa Regala Garcia

Trap Building 56
Charmaine Chan

Teaching What You Know 58
Maria Gliceria Valdez

House Dog 60
Alastair Wee

Dark Alley 61
Ong Chao Hong

Inspired 62
Alaka Rajan Skinner

A Ravaged Body 63
James Tan

Dying To See 64
Moses Sia

Albularyo 66
Jeff David

Strong 68
Claire Betita de Guzman

The Musician 70
Chinie Hidalgo Diaz

Never the Flesh Forever 72
Danny Jalil

My Everything 73
Rizza Corella Punsalan

The Price of Belief 74
Victor Fernando R. Ocampo

Underground Identity 76
Ho See Kum

I Have a Secret! 77
Glenn Russel D. Alejon

Orange 78
Z.L. Mercado

Three 80
Jenny Faith Koh

Anxiety 82
Anngee Neo

**If Travis Bickle had been
a Singaporean** 83
Francis Lau

Otterly Gorgeous 84
Danielle Lim

Computer Hang   85
Don Low

Jump   86
Janet Hui Ching Tay

If I Die   88
Rajendiran Suresh

Christmas Mourn   89
Chris Ramos

Draconian   90
Judy Tham

Answer the Question   92
Daniel Seifert

Into The Light   94
Therese Jamora-Garceau

Room for One   96
Selene Estaris

Hermit GPT   98
Cheah Sinann

Storefronts   99
Michaela Benedicto

Visiting   100
Zed Yeo

In an Instance   102
Veronica Leow

Screaming Woman   103
Loh Guan Liang

Acceptance   104
Paul Eric Roca

Messages   105
Rosanna Licari

P(X)   106
Dennis Yeo

Pick-up   108
May Tobias-Papa

Manifest   109
Myrza Sison

Dandelion   110
Tan Ai Qi

Breast   112
Greth Barredo

Auntie Clutter   114
Quek Hong Shin

Liddat Also Can   115
Clara Mok

Something Wonderful   116
Dawn Ho

The Rose   117
Tan Suet Lee

The Hustle   118
Patrick Sagaram

Ellen's Secret   120
John Evan P. Orias

Digging out the Truth   122
Twisstii

The Proposal   123
Kat Chua

Nipa Hut   124
Euginia Tan

Love Missed   126
Audrey Tay

Infinite Chances   127
Rye Antonio

The Hum   128
Margaret Tang

Fish Bowl   130
Melissa Salva

Feline Sovereignty   132
Peter Loh

Velvet   133
Carmie Ortego

First Love   134
Rosie Wee

Monorail   136
Daren Shiau

Girl, Gilded   137
Andy Lopez

Always   138
Eli Ampil Gagelonia

Missing Things   139
NY Chua

Transient   140
John Gilford Auxilio Doquila

Packages   142
Inez Tan

**The Consequence of Uncontrolled
Shopping in 2020**   144
Arif Rafhan

Maggie, Me, and the Ducati   145
Verena Tay

Shoegaze Girl   146
Ian Rosales Casocot

Wifi Password   148
Daryll Fay Gayatin

Window   149
Clement Wee

Woke   150
Felix Cheong and Clio Ding

How We End   151
Amy Chia

Space Oddity   152
Jocelyn Low

Big Day   154
Chan Ziqian

Living in the Moment   155
Alan Bay

And Then   156
Noelle Q. de Jesus

The Ghost Marriage   158
Dave Chua

Playback   160
Yeo Wei Wei

Love and its New Forms   162
Sara Florian

An Affair   165
Angelo R. Lacuesta

Afterword   166
Felix Cheong

Acknowledgements   168

Preface

Noelle Q. de Jesus
Co-Editor

A lifetime ago she studied writing in flat, windy Ohio. For her Techniques of Fiction class, the professor used *Sudden Fiction*, Shapard and Thomas's very first anthology. She fell in love.

This is the way we tell stories, she thought. Brief. No explanations. Almost like a joke.

Over 12 years, she pitched, curated, and published two books of flash fiction in the Philippines. And she never stopped reading or writing it, loving it even more.

Last year, she had a notion: It's time for a collection from the region—stories even shorter—spare, subtle, and surprising—the way Asians tell stories. She asked a friend, a renowned Singaporean writer, with more experience and books beneath his belt, to be co-editor.

Let's make it a little different, he said. Let's have graphic fiction, too.

They talked for three hours over coffee, running into first one title and then another by sheer serendipity. He spoke to his publisher, and then they all met in a chat group.

People face an immensity of content every day on multiple screens and their attention spans are seemingly growing in reverse. Microfiction (300 words or less) just makes sense, they argued. We weep and we grieve. We laugh and engage. We learn and are enlightened. Our hearts move with joy or insight or catharsis. We are undone by what we see, what we miss and realise only later, the connections, but also the missed connections. And the exquisite arrangement of story elements on one single page can be transforming.

And thus, they were off. The stories flew in like wild birds bearing small gifts. She read with surprise. With wonder. Again, her epiphany: small is powerful, and true love endures. (283 words)

Resurrection
Jose Y. Dalisay

It had been at least thirty years since his hands had brushed a typewriter's keyboard, but once he pressed the first few keys it all came back to him—the poised fingers, the thrill of imprinting words on paper with nothing else coming in between. Of course the words could be erased or crossed out, but until someone took the trouble, they were practically indelible, there for as long as the paper itself endured. He typed a word that he had not seen or used for a very long time, from a class in Elizabethan drama— "farthingale"—and marvelled at its resurrection in Vogue pica.

The Vogue sans serif font was the reason he had paid a hefty price for this woodgrain Royal from 1929. Typewriters were out of his usual collecting range—he favoured Bakelite clocks and radios—but he had learned that Vogue was among the rarest and most stylish of typewriter fonts, its lean letters as chic as a flapper raising a cocktail glass. He would type letters in it to friends, pretending that a depression and a war had yet to happen and that people were happily guzzling forbidden whisky.

The Royal had come in a battered case all the way from Petula, Minnesota. It was full of dings and scratches, and he noticed that a name had been typed and taped inside the case: "A. Hansen." He wondered what "A" meant—Abel, Anthony, Ambrose? Amanda? He tried as many variants as he could on Google, until he stumbled on Agnetha Hansen, a Swedish immigrant who had learned to write poetry in English.

She had lain her three children in the snow before jumping off a bridge. She had typed a farewell poem. The words in the photocopy spoke to him in Vogue. (297 words)

Jose Y. Dalisay has published over 40 books of fiction and nonfiction. His second novel, *Soledad's Sister*, was shortlisted for the inaugural Man Asian Literary Prize in 2007 and has been published in Philippine, Italian, French, and American editions. He is Professor Emeritus of English at the University of the Philippines.

Parenthood
Diana Mandac

Her doll-like frame shrank into itself, chin wobbling, moony eyes glazed with chunky tears, hands clumsily grasping the air, reaching for me.

"Why did you do it?" I asked, hands clasped, indignant, huffing for breath, trying to keep the word vomit from spilling.

"I'm sorry, I was still a child," Mama replied. (52 words)

Diana Mandac is a BA Language and Literature student at University of the Philippines Baguio. Her interests include poetry, writing, anime, and manga. Like her fellow Gen Zs, she was raised by the Internet and her attention span is limited to one-minute reels.

The Painting
Vicky Chong

Ling had already started packing when I arrived. The eyes above her mask were red and swollen. "Dust!" she explained, but I knew better. The eldest of three girls, she had lived in this house the longest. During the last months of Mother's life, she had moved back to nurse her, so I understood the attachment. I had moved to Australia for university and settled there. Maggie, the middle child, did not bother to return home from England where she now lived. "There is nothing in that house for me. Feel free to take whatever you want," she said. The dilapidated semi-detached, as well as anything of value, were to be sold and the proceeds split amongst us three sisters.

I eyed the Chinese ink painting on the wall. I recognised the red seal. This was the late artist's earlier piece before he established his trademark of minimalism that made him famous. The auctioneer in Hong Kong had confirmed its authenticity from the photos I had sent him and estimated the painting to be worth six figures.

"Daddy's favourite painting," Ling said as she stood beside me.

My heart pounded. "Are we selling this? Together with those crystals?"

"Don't be silly. Too much hassle to list on Carousell. If you want, just take them."

"What were you intending to do with them?" I asked lightly.

"Donate to the church for their annual bazaar." She started putting cookbooks into cartons.

"Could I have it?'

"Take them. Mummy's favourite crystal ware would fit in your Australian bungalow more than my HDB flat."

"I meant this painting.'

Her eyes widened.

"I want something of Dad as a memento."

Her eyes moistened, her smile reminding me of Mummy.
"Of course. Take it."

I swallowed the lump of guilt in my throat and smiled back.

(300 words)

Vicky Chong is the author of *Racket and Other Stories*. Her short story, "The Uber Driver", won third prize in the 2018 Nick Joaquin Literary Awards Asia-Pacific. Other short stories are found in the anthologies, *The Best Asian Short Stories*, in 2021 and 2022, *Letter to My Son* and *A View of Stars*.

Curry Puffs
Paul GnanaSelvam

The event of the past night has left a glob of air in my throat. Groggily, I reverse the car and start driving to work in the light drizzle. At the little curb where I need to make a turn stands Appa, an imposing figure now eaten by age, clad in baggy shorts and T-shirt struggling to hold his umbrella straight. His other hand precariously holds something close to his chest. It is hard to believe that this quiet, laidback, sedentary man takes a menacing avatar after his evening shot of whiskey. Intoxicated, his throat and lungs expanded into a deafening avalanche of misgivings, self-pity and revenge laced with atrocious verbosity. I belch. Thosai and mint-chutney breath from breakfast intervenes with Mum's words: "It wasn't him. It was the bottle." I stop and wind down the window. Appa stoops down laboriously, his glossy eyes peering through his rusty gold-framed glasses. "Shall I send you home?" I ask. He shakes his head. I pinch my temples. I deliberate upon an apology but wait for words to avail. "Take these," he instructs. "Drive safe," he bids before turning to leave. After a hard day's work, it's only fair I am warranted some peace and quiet. Appa went overboard last night, shouting profanities at the porch in full view of the neighbours. When decent pleading did not work, I had to chastise him, just like what he did when I was a child. I found a stack of newspapers, rolled them up and whacked him on his back to subdue him from his trance. In a flash, the roaring lion turned into a mewing kitten. Peace, at last. I look into the pink plastic bag. It yields two curry-puffs, warm. A parent's heart is soft as dew, a child's hard as rain. (299 words)

Paul GnanaSelvam is an Ipoh-born writer and poet whose work focuses on the Indian diaspora. His first book, *Latha's Christmas & Other Stories* was published in 2013, while *The Elephant Trophy & Other Stories* was published by Penguin Random House SEA in 2021. He lectures at Universiti Teknologi MARA (Perak Campus), Malaysia.

Birdsong
Chen Cuifen

My mother recorded the sound of the *oo-oo* bird for me when I went to Birmingham to study. Other Singaporean mothers got cup noodles and Prima laksa paste for their kids. Mine said, *you can buy those things from Chinatown, but you won't hear this stupid bird.* I set it as my alarm tone so I'd continue associating it with annoyance. One time, I forgot to turn it off for the weekend, and the boy I was sleeping with that winter asked me *what the hell is that* when my phone started blaring at 7am, *OO-OO, OO-OO.* I could have taught him about Southeast Asian cuckoos. Showed him a picture of the koel with its red eyes, said, *the sound of home.* What I said was, *the sound of my mother's love.* He laughed. *Some kind of love, eh.* I laughed too, because he was right, and he'd never know what it meant to me, to be loved in such an ugly and cacophonous way; to be a fledgling in a foreign nest, eating food that isn't meant for me. *Yes*, I said. I bit off syllables, sanded down their sharp edges against tongue and teeth. Swallowed the sunburnt bits that were mine alone so only pretty noises came out of my mouth. *When I go home for summer, I'll make sure to tell her.* (225 words)

Chen Cuifen is a writer from Singapore. She was the winner of the Troubadour International Poetry Prize 2018, the Literary Taxidermy Short Story Competition 2019, and most recently received an Honourable Mention in the Golden Point Award 2021. She loves coffee, liminal spaces, and fantastic things.

What I Learned from Mum
Dora Tan

You can't eat it, but it tastes bitter. It smells like sour grass. Even when I'm not holding it, the smell is there. It's everywhere in the house. I don't like the smell, but I don't not like it. I'm used to it. It's like how bakers get used to the smell of bread that they don't smell it anymore.

Mum is in the kitchen cooking. One hand gripping the wok, the other holding a metal spatula, fiercely frying clanging the wok. Even from the living room, I can see the sweat and scowl on her face. She gives a shout. Both Su and I rush for the pack. The first one who reaches it gets to do it. It's fun! It's the only time I get to use matches without being scolded.

I grab the Salem first so I get to light it. I put one in my mouth and feel very grown-up. The problem is I'm not very good at striking matches. I break the first and second match. I succeed with the third, but the fan blows it out. Mum gets angry. "Where is it? Why are you taking so long!" I can't answer because I have something in my mouth, and I get more nervous and waste another match.

It's not that easy for a seven-year-old. The timing has to be right. I have to suck just when the flame is at the tip. Sometimes I have to suck twice if it doesn't "catch" the first time, which makes me cough, because I would swallow smoke. Finally, it catches, the tip glows orange like magic. I exhale the smoke, go to the kitchen, put it in Mum's mouth. (282 words)

Dora Tan is most known for her plays which include *A Wedding, A Funeral and Lucky the Fish* (2020, 2014) and *I'm Fine Really* (2020). Her short stories include *Seven Views of Redhill* (podcast 2021, staged 2019). She won the National Arts Council's Golden Point Award in 2015 (3rd) and 2007 (2nd).

Showbusiness
Charina Mercado

Her mother taps her shoulder needlessly. Sheila is already awake. Baby Jackjack has been crying since midnight, rousing the neighbours spitting distance away.

"Please," her mother begs. "He's so hungry. You don't have to get the milk, I can."

"How much?"

"A box of formula is now five hundred pesos."

The wall clock advertising cheap gin, shows it's so late no one will notice.

In the bathroom, Sheila thinks. She's in fifth grade, but her math is weak.

The photo of herself swimming in the river earned two hundred pesos. Five hundred is more than double that. What would be worth double?

Her mother has already put out the same question to the world. A man so nearsighted, his nose dominates the laptop screen, answers with words that sound like swish-swish. Her mother understands him perfectly.

"She can do that. No problem, sir."

She pulls Sheila by the arm to a circle drawn on the floor, muttering, "Do the dance!" The cellphone is already perched on top of the ironing board.

Brows furrowed as she focuses on the choreography, Sheila wiggles her arms to pulsating music. Her mother edges in beside her, an arm briefly darting into the lens's view, as she tugs her daughter's nightgown.

"It's hot, you'll be sweating. Better take this off." Sheila swats her mother's hand away.

A loud banging at the door startles everyone. The cellphone clatters to the floor and is kicked out of sight.

"Go to bed, Sheila," her mother snaps. At the door, her mother talks to the barrio captain.

"Nothing going on here, Cap. Just putting the baby to sleep."

As if on cue, Jackjack wails again. (276 words)

Charina Mercado produces comics on online sexual abuse and exploitation of Filipino children. The comics are given away in public schools to educate children about what constitutes abuse. In 2021, Mercado wrote *Other People's Children* on the legal, emotional and social processes involved in adopting a Filipino child.

I'm Coming to Help You
Wesley Leon Aroozoo

Wesley Leon Aroozoo is a multidisciplinary artist from 13 Little Pictures with works that span across literary arts, film, television, performance and theatre. His works have been awarded and nominated at the Busan International Film Festival, Singapore Book Awards, and the Epigram Books Fiction Prize.

Crossing The Rice Field
Shinnen Cahandig

It was four in the morning when I heard the clanging of the metal on the frying pan—an alarm clock for me and my siblings. As I put my shoes inside my bag, my mother prepared the ice box, filling it with ice candy she would sell at school. When the clock struck five, it was time to walk across the wide rice field bathed in the morning dew.

"Oh, your father didn't tell me; we should've taken the other way," Mother said.

We removed our slippers, rolled up our pants, and dipped our feet in the mud without stepping on the tadpoles. "The mud is cold! Like snow but brownish," my brother said happily. We were thankful the mud didn't hide any sharp bamboo or hard stones that might wound our feet. The pink eggs of snails clung to rotting sticks that stood in the chocolate field. Illuminated by the morning sun, they beamed like crystals. My little sister picked them up and held them in her palm. "I'll trade this for money, so we can be rich," she whispered to me. (184 words)

Shinnen Cahandig was born in Bugabungan Upi, Maguindanao and currently resides in Davao City. She is a student at the University of Southeastern Philippines, taking a Bachelor of Arts in Literature and Cultural Studies. Her hobbies include creating digital artwork and painting.

The Cynical Sisters
Rachel Tey

"So, the nuns are from Africa?" I ask. My mother and I have stopped at a red light, and she squints at the GPS on her phone. She's antsy whenever she suspects she's taken a wrong turn.

"Mummy?"

"What?" she snaps. "No, they're not, why would the Cenacle Sisters be Africans?"

"But Senegal's in Africa."

"My God, Vicky," she scoffs, as the light turns green.

"'Cenacle' means the room of the Last Supper."

"Didn't the Last Supper take place in Jerusalem?" She sighs. "Just talk to the nuns, okay?"

"Suppose they don't believe a word I have to say?"

"Why wouldn't they?"

"Because they're cynical?"

I persist. "The Cynical Sisters?"

Silence.

Later I find myself sitting in a wicker chair facing a sister whose name I forget immediately after she says it. It's a name only a nun would have, like Sister Perpetua of the Holy Transfiguration.

"Sister Perpetua" has downward-sloping eyes, the kindly sort that stare at me with pity.

Nothing we discuss leaves an impression, except for her parting words. As I get up to go, she asks how one can remain in the darkness of the tomb when our Christ had resurrected.

Back in the car, I tell my mother I'm never speaking with a nun again. Not until I have some philosophical or theological chops under my belt.

"Don't say I didn't try, Vicky," is her steely response. "Didn't I care enough to drive you to a godforsaken corner of Jurong? Haven't I done my part?"

I think I have an answer, but again, words fail me. There's an emptiness in my chest, amplified by the stuffiness of the tomb "Sister Perpetua" has put me in.

I wonder if I'll emerge by Easter Sunday. (288 words)

Rachel Tey is the author of the *Tea in Pajamas* series and the short story, "The Midnight Mission". She is an editorial director, part-time university lecturer, and creative writing instructor. Rachel is looking to publish her new novella on memory, and to travel more with her husband and two kids.

White Jade, White Elephant
Claire A. Miranda

By the time Serena and Conrad agreed on the auspicious pairing of red and beach sand for the dining room walls, Serena realised she must give up her work as a writer. Conrad, meanwhile, had taken to consulting the list of do's and don'ts the feng shui master on Temple Street had prescribed to gain business luck and happiness. These included: reorienting the king-sized bed in the bedroom, suspending gold tokens above the balcony doors, and positioning a snarling black and gold lion— the ugliest lump of plaster Serena had ever seen— in the northwest corner of the study. And because Conrad instructed it, Serena began lighting pink candles whenever he travelled for business. Conrad also surprised her with a dragon carved out of white jade, obscenely priced, insisting Serena keep it on the desk where she did her writing, to counter the flow of negative energies. To keep his mum in good health for the next five years, Conrad gifted the older woman with pearls for the Lunar New Year. It was the Year of the Tiger—Conrad was born a Tiger—so he did all in his power to dispel the disastrous Five Yellow hovering in several places on his chart. Once the dining room walls had dried, Serena pushed all the furniture into place and set a tabletop fountain in the northwest corner of the flat. She was taking photos to share on Instagram when the phone call came. Conrad's mum had passed that very hour. That's when Serena tossed the hideous lion down the chute, then rearranged the sofa and armchairs the way she wanted. The jade dragon she put on eBay. Today she would write and not stop, despite the master's admonitions that her career choice would have ruinous results. (295 words)

Claire A. Miranda is a documentary producer living in Manila. Born in the Philippines and raised in Chicago, Illinois, she also holds roots in Seattle, Melbourne, and Singapore.

The People on My Boat
Reanne Mak

When I agreed to help them, I was only aware that two families were escaping. But I sat like a shepherd looking over twenty-two souls, huddled together like penguins in winter. Their wet clothes clung tightly to their bodies, ragged and torn from scrambling through bushes in hope of not getting caught. All was silent except the sound of the sea as the neon yellow life-vests illuminated in the black of night, as every pair of deep dark eyes closed for a nap, only to be jolted awake when the same screams and cries rang through their heads, as traumatised children, crying mothers, lonely husbands, and fading souls, stared into the vast ocean. Who knew what they were thinking? My boat sailed on into the peaceful night, but I knew their fears were drowning them. Those were the people on my boat. (142 words)

Reanne Mak is an avid reader and has loved writing since young. Participating in various events and attaining many achievements has only further developed her passion and interest.

Huawei Rescue

Maya Calica Collins

Maya Calica Collins is a Filipino writer, illustrator, and storyteller based in New Zealand. She has published three books, and currently runs an art teaching business in Auckland. During the lockdowns, she spent one hundred days writing, drawing and animating stories as Maya the three-minute storyteller. For more, check out mayacalica.com.

New Year's Resolution

Suraya Md Nasir

Suraya Md Nasir received her PhD in 2019 from Kyoto Seika University, majoring in manga theory. She currently teaches at Universiti Pendidikan Sultan Ismail. Under her pseudonym Jonsuraya, she is a comic artist behind the series *Jejon Di Jepun* (2015-continuing). She is also involved in the pre-production of animated cartoon series as writer and creative director, such as her 2D animated title, *Misi Ady.* in 2015.

Inheritance
Cherrie Sing

You dance around the grand wooden table that once belonged to your father. Secretly, of course, away from the prying eyes of your employees. "All mine," you whisper, as you giddily bask in the glory of being the boss.

Your brothers never had a chance. Foolish of them to expect anything in the family business when they had been away so many years. Sure, Father had instructed that they should be given money as part of the business he had built. Yet Father passed on without a will, leaving everything to you. In good blind faith that you would follow his wishes.

It only took two terse sentences to keep your siblings silent: "I have no money to pay your shares. I will pay you in goods."

Dismay etched your brothers' faces. What use were goods when they now lived overseas? How entitled of them! Without a choice, they gave up everything. Went back to their foreign homes without a fight. Their only parting words: "Take care of our sister."

They should have taken her with them. If they cared so much.

Sister was an expense. Sure, she had cooked, taken care of Father, cleaned house—but you could have easily hired maids for that sort of work. She also checked the accounts of the company—a job you will have to take out of her hands soon. Harder to drag her out of the family home, but if anyone can, you can. Hahaha. Evil you. What could she do but cry? Because if anyone deserved the company, it was you. Father loved you the least. You should get everything as compensation.

Fine grey dust blows through the open windows of your office, coating the table. You have Father's blessing. (290 words)

Cherrie Sing is a Filipino-Chinese writer based in Manila. She was a fellow in two national workshops: Siliman Writing Workshop and Iligan Writing Workshop. Her work has been published in local and international magazines and anthologies, most recently, in *Unsaid: An Asian Anthology*.

Each Other
Yvette Fernandez

Till they were 11, Nanay dressed Mameng and Patring alike. No one could tell them apart.

But Mameng grew up to be the lithe dancer who fell asleep over her algebra homework. And Patring was the honours student with bruises on her hips and thighs from bumping into table corners and door knobs.

The only thing they had in common was the boy they loved in their 20s, and he broke their hymens and their hearts.

"Please get along," Nanay cried whenever they bickered, after Tatay had died and she, too, had little time left. "You'll only have each other when I'm gone."

The few times their paths crossed during their working years, the sisters had nothing much to say to each other, and didn't even have anything to fight about anymore.

On their 65th birthday, a widowed Mameng was feted with a dance party by her son who lived far away with a woman she disdained. Patring wasn't there. She treated her university colleagues to dinner at a Chinese restaurant.

They each went home alone to empty shells of spaces.

One sticky summer a decade and a half later, thereabouts, Mameng was roused by a call from their old neighbourhood. Patring had been found wandering the streets again, half-dressed, and this time, she had defecated in public. Mameng had no other recourse but to take her twin home with her.

That night, a just bathed Patring picked up an invisible telephone.

"Nanay, we're here," Patring whispered to their dead mother. "Yes, yes. We're finally with each other."

Mameng pushed herself up from her armchair, and steadied herself with her walker. She hobbled over to the couch and ran a comb through her sister's brittle hair. (286 words)

Yvette Fernandez is the chief storyteller at one of the Philippines' largest conglomerates. Previously, she was editor-in-chief at *Esquire* and *Town&Country* Philippines, and an editor at Bloomberg News in New York. She has a master's degree in Journalism from Columbia University. She's written over a dozen children's books.

A Feast For Neneng
Nixie E. Serna

Loloy dresses his little sister in her finest dress—the finest, for it's the only one she owns. Their mother is up early to play cards with the neighbours in hopes of doubling their money to buy food, but most of the time, she returns in the afternoon with less change in her pockets, while their debt to the sari-sari store next door grows another inch. Loloy cannot remember when his father last returned home.

Holding his sister's hand, Loloy looks left and right before crossing the street. His sister has not yet learned to navigate the streets on her own, but soon she will. She has to. Loloy learned how to cross the street when he was her age.

Soon, the siblings reach the tall buildings with huge posters of food that make both their stomachs grumble. They stop in front of a giant red bee.

"Happy birthday, Neneng! What do you want to eat?" Loloy asks.

Neneng looks up at her brother with excitement, but quickly looks down. She picks at a stray thread of her dress.

"Don't worry," he coaxes his hesitant sister. "You can have anything you want."

Neneng's eyes linger on the restaurant. She finally says in a small voice, "Fried chicken and spaghetti and burger."

Loloy smiles at her, revealing his missing front teeth. "Stay here," he directs her into the shadow cast by a blue car in the parking lot. "Don't go anywhere. I won't be long." She nods and sits on a curb. He circles to the back of the building where bags of trash are piled up like a mountain. He dives into one of the open bags. Loloy makes sure that they will have a feast tonight. (287 words)

Nixie E. Serna is a BA English (Creative Writing) student at the University of the Philippines Mindanao. When not writing, she can be found drawing, dreaming, petting cats, or listening to EXO.

We Played with Same Dolls but Invented Our Own Games

Anisha Ralhan

Yours waved like a pageant, posed in bridal red, listened to heartbeats with a tiny stethoscope. Mine sailed paper boats in puddles, brought home lice and stolen lemons.

Ma says you were always an easy child. First to finish your greens, ever ready to mingle, happy with your hand-me-downs. Unlike me, you never got into trouble with the authorities. Straight A's even in your teens.

I knew then we were never going to be sisters who correct each other's cat eyes, invent alibis, nurse broken hearts; twin on TikTok. So, I clenched my secrets till my fist hurt. Hid my marksheet under the mattress, wept in locked bathrooms, kissed a boy only to taste regret.

I was fourteen and you were twelve the night you were first rushed to the ER. Your face a two-week-old party balloon. Ma didn't get any sleep that year. I wondered, *what if this were me?*

You grew up with inhalers and steroids. The weight gain, the hair loss somehow felt like it was all my fault. We started fighting a lot. Over the remote control, Ma's affection, the better room, then boys.

We changed hairstyles, countries, jobs, partners. Drifting into each other's lives unceremoniously on birthdays and festivals. We communicate via carefully crafted texts, occasionally with cat memes.

Henna-glazed hands twist the doorknob. I slip into the room, and find you, looking regal in bridal red, just as I expected. The dresser is covered in powder and glitter. Velvet boxes with mouths half-open.

"Ready for the big day?"

Your brows are furrowed.

You place the long necklace on my palms, staring at two tight knots near the clasp.

I study this gilded mess closely. Curl my fingers around the edges, thinking if I am able to fix this, maybe I'll fix everything. (297 words)

Anisha Ralhan is a freelance copywriter based in Singapore. She has a master's degree in Creative Writing from Goldsmiths, University of London. Her work has been published in *The Best Asian Short Stories 2022, What We Inherit, QLRS* and more. She thinks of herself as a cat-whisperer, but Mowgli, her cat, disagrees. Get in touch with her at anisharalhan.com.

Found Wanting
Abigail C. James

Baste kept remembering white Tinang and the day Papa had pulled the calf from her backside onto the dusty earth. That was when he still lived in their *kubo* up on the mountain. He asked Papa if that was how he was born from Mama. Papa laughed his angry laugh before pinching Baste's arm until it went red.

That was before Mama left and came back with a big belly to bring Baste to the city. She took Baste away from Papa in a shiny black car. She said he would have a new daddy – Daddy Doug (*always call him Daddy*). Mama said Daddy Doug would not hurt Baste like Papa did. She said Daddy Doug would send him to a nice school. She said Daddy Doug would buy him shoes and toys. She did not say Daddy Doug was a pink man with yellow teeth and white hair.

When baby Alan came, Mama was too busy to play with Baste. On the first day of school, the other kids teased him because he was dark-skinned and could not speak English. They called him *taga-bukid*. He climbed up on the highest tree at school to maybe see his house on the mountain top. The guard saw him and shouted for him to come down. It was getting dark. *Where are your parents? Your yaya?* the guard asked. Baste could only shake his head.

He sat near the guardhouse as the sun went down over the shadows of his real home. He thought about Tinang and the calf. He thought about Papa and his heavy hands. He thought about Daddy Doug who laid no hands on him nor his pale blue eyes either. And he thought about Mama who had left him once and then again. (295 words)

Abigail C. James is from Cagayan de Oro, Philippines. Her works have appeared in the *Carayan Journal, Tinubdan New Voices from Northern Mindanao*, and *Dx Machina 4: Literature in the Time of COVID-19*. She teaches English at Xavier University-Ateneo de Cagayan.

Love Child
Gem Deveras Mañosa

I was sixteen, alone in a car with a boy. He told me a dirty secret.

"I know your dad. He has another kid...my cousin."

I jumped out of the car and threw my cigarette butt at his windshield.

Dad died when I was twenty-two. At the wake, a woman accosted me.

"I'm looking for the daughter of ..."

"That's me."

"His other daughter..."

"Get out of here," I hissed.

Today is Dad's 80th, and I decide to commemorate the occasion on FB. Even if he won't ever see it.

A prompt appears: People You Might Know. A gallery of photos. I scroll and I see her. My sister. *Half*-sister. With Dad's last name under her face. I search for signs of my father, of me. Nothing. No one will ever think we're related.

Her page opens before my eyes.

She is married to the cousin of my college classmate. She has two sons. A photo: the four of them wearing identical dive suits. I recognise the island behind the boat. I was there a year ago with my family. A video: her child shooting a winning basket. I gasp. It is my son's school.

I marvel at the number of our Mutual Friends. I wonder why they didn't tell me about her.

She studied in a Catholic school. She lives in Parañaque. She has a catering business. She has 1,594 Friends.

She lived my life.

My cursor hovers: Add Friend. I shudder. I shrug. Then I click on the Home button instead. I attach a photo of me as a newborn. With Dad, gazing down at my face, beaming. Full of love.

Happy birthday in heaven, Daddy. I love you forever. Your girl.

I click Post. (287 words)

Gem Deveras Mañosa is a wife and mother. She enjoys crocheting, long walks, and listening to audiobooks for hours. She wrote a biography about her father-in-law, *Bobby: Francisco Mañosa, An Intimate Portrait* (Tukod, 2021), and is part of the anthology, *Life in a Flash* (UST, 2022).

Home and My Lot
Libay Linsangan Cantor

When my father told her that we could have the lot, the one they were reserving for me as a sort of inheritance slash build-your-house-on-it-if-you-want, so she could build a house on it, supposedly for us—she and I, to live as a couple for eternity—my mind went blank. And you know what? So did my heart.

It's the kind of blank that stares you in the face. The kind writers dread on a deadline day. The type that leaves you alone during times of distress and duress. That kind of blank.

In between puffs, they were planning our lives. Mine and hers. But I never wanted to be part of it.

She was telling my father how she had accumulated enough to build a dream house for us. How she has earned enough in her career—one that I wholly support—to realise this life she wants. Never mind if she doesn't fully support mine or looks down on my career choices, belittling mine compared to hers. I mean, sure, I write news and movie reviews for a living. But hey, nothing beats litigating for farmers displaced from their lands. You win, dear, you win.

I didn't realise this was a contest.

Of course, she had to use her legal mind to present another dilemma: how to title the property. If it's my lot but her house, how do we go about it? Never mind that we still don't have the legality to recognise our union. In this country, we never will, at least in our lifetime. But legalities aside, what concerned me most is the picture they're painting of our future.

Just a snapshot. I never see myself in it. Never.

Because I never felt at home with her. Ever. (293 words)

Libay Linsangan Cantor is a two-time winner of the Don Carlos Palanca Memorial Awards for Literature for her fiction in Filipino. A former media practitioner and film educator, she currently works as a language localisation professional servicing global brands like Duolingo and Netflix. Email her at libay.cantor@gmail.com.

Those Left Behind
Gene Tamesis, Jr.

Her younger brother signed up for two marathons. One was virtual, to raise awareness of pancreatic cancer. The other was Boston, the holy grail of marathons, where one had to be superhuman to qualify, or super lucky to win the lottery for race slots. He was neither superhuman nor super lucky, but he decided this year to try again.

Her older sister walked to the beach every day. From her house, the California coast was fifteen minutes from door to shore. With nothing but her journal and phone, she was out the door as soon as her daughter left for school. Everyone knew where to find her as she left a trail of modern-day breadcrumbs on Instagram and in three different chat groups. She wondered how far she could walk in a year.

Her older brother read books on the Spanish Armada. The crumbling of superpowers in history had a soothing effect on him. "Did you know that —?" little snippets of history peppered their family chat group, and everyone knew the next one was on its way. He had a stack of history books waiting by his bedside.

Her youngest sister said nothing. She went to work every day, as she always had for the past thirty years, and went home promptly at six. She was in bed by ten. She felt the best way to lose herself was in everyday routine.

Her mother woke up sobbing. By noon, she forgot what happened. And by evening, she would remember and start sobbing again.

And she? She watched them all. All at once. She figured it was another game of hide and seek. But she found them all, no matter how hard they tried to hide. (286 words)

Gene Tamesis, Jr. grew up in Manila but has built a career in marketing throughout Southeast Asia. Today, he lives in Jakarta, Indonesia working for one of the leading digital job platforms in the region. He enjoys writing, drawing, running, swimming, and exploring the islands of Indonesia with his wife and three children.

Curating Life and Death
Dengcoy Miel

Dengcoy Miel is a cartoonist by day and becomes a dark, brooding figure at night looming the landscape. Then he paints.

Sweet Release
Risa Regala Garcia

I was aware of the sound of nothing, cocooned in semi-darkness as my other senses engaged. A warm, buttery sensation enveloped my back. I took a moment to relish the impending pleasure.

Getting a home-service massage in the middle of the workweek was a luxury, but I had been under stress. Marco was off drinking with a friend, and I had the house to myself.

I had found the spa service on Marco's phone a few days before, as he went for massages quite frequently. "Angela" was beside the spa's name, so I requested her. She arrived in an hour. It wasn't long before I felt the bombardment of her warm hands, kneading my feet, squeezing my calves, pushing on my thighs and hips. I grunted in protest, but the assault continued.

"My husband Marco told me about you," I whispered to Angela as she ground her knuckles into my nape.

No answer. Perhaps she didn't hear me.

She had me turn face down on the bed. I closed my eyes as my pain slowly melted away, then dozed off. I woke up to the sound of voices—one of them was Marco's.

"You're married?" Angela hissed at my husband from above my head.

I felt a chill.

Her warm hands cupped my face ever-so-gently, and as they wrenched my head to the left, I waited for the sweet release.

"No! No! Oh God, please don't," I heard Marco scream.

The last sound I heard was a snap. (248 words)

Risa Regala Garcia began writing stories at six years old. She has attended classes with Professor Emeritus Cristina P. Hidalgo and has contributed articles to several local publications. In 2011, her essays were published in the book, *Turning Points: Women in Transit*. She currently writes with a group under Dr Rofel G. Brion.

Trap Building
Charmaine Chan

"It's so nice having you back," Naomi said. "With just the three of us together again."

Only their mother could tuck a barb into such an innocuous sentence. And do it as elegantly as she did. But both her children knew her well enough to know it was there. Under the table, Ruth grabbed her brother's hand and squeezed it in a death grip.

Don't rise to it.

The warning was taken. "Nothing like family, right?" Jesse said lightly. Naomi smiled at him, letting his deliberate equivocation slide.

Ruth felt something twist inside her as she looked at her brother, holding his fork so tightly his knuckles were white. It wasn't fair, she thought. She so rarely got to see him, but when she did, she was never able to fully enjoy his company. His uneasy dynamic with their mother constantly fed the tension that coiled like a snake in the pit of her stomach.

It hadn't always been this way. She couldn't remember when Jesse had changed from golden child to black sheep. Was there a moment in time when she could have done something? Her only consolation was that she'd gotten better at managing the relationship through the years, honing the techniques of diffusion, of distraction, of diversion to a high art.

What she had not yet learned was how not to let it get to her. For Ruth had not yet grown a protective carapace and every quarrel still stung like a blow, felt like a personal failure. Watching them chafe and rub against each other, sometimes drawing blood, was often more than she could bear.

The fact that they loved one another made it somehow worse, made it cruel, made it incomprehensible. (286 words)

Formerly a lawyer, Charmaine Chan is a writer and editor from Singapore, with work in *Her World, The Peak* and *Prestige*. Her poetry is published in *No Other City: The Ethos Anthology of Urban Poetry*, and her memoir, *The Magic Circle* (Ethos Books 2018), was shortlisted for the 2018 Singapore Literature Prize. She lives in Melbourne, Australia.

Teaching What You Know
Maria Gliceria Valdez

You were excited to teach what you know.

The first poem you made your senior high school students read was "Soledad" by Angela Manalang Gloria. You first asked how TV shows portrayed mistresses. The most frequent answer was the word *igat*. That word made your skin tingle. You remembered how that word, which is the Bisaya for slut, pertained to you.

At that time, you didn't know that when you let your lover kiss you in the wee hours of morning, making sure you went home before the sun came up, he would wash remnants of you off his skin and send a good morning text to his girlfriend. You just wanted to feel needed—someone must really need you when they go through all the trouble to keep you a secret.

You decided to teach Eve Ensler's "Vagina Monologues" instead. The students are too young for this material, your High School Coordinator said. How could learners have an age limit, when abuse victims do not? You were happy the girls in the class felt empowered and felt comfortable in their own skin. Even the boys stood up along with them.

You are their teacher, the coordinator said. You should know what you are teaching them. They should be taught self-respect and not show skin. *Kaya sila nare*-rape, the coordinator said, looking smug. You thought of how you loved wearing baggy pants and still, your ex-boyfriend tore them off you, like you deprived him of something. You thought to yourself, maybe you weren't fit to teach. What do you know, really?

At the end of the class, some girls approached you and thanked you. This made you smile. You were finally a teacher. So, you continue to teach, and maybe learn things as you go. (295 words)

Maria Gliceria Valdez currently teaches in the Department of Humanities in the University of Philippines. Her short stories, poems, and essays are published in *Tingle: Anthology of Pinay Lesbian Writing*, *Dx Machina: Literature in the Time of COVID-19*, and *Press:100 Love Letters*. She was born and raised in Davao City, the Philippines.

House Dog
Alastair Wee

There's an old man at the park who shouts at dogs. Red cap, bandaged hands. Every night at ten, he shuffles in, smelling like Marlboro and a pack of six. A dachshund yips and he rounds on it. *Kan ni na*, he curses, loud at range, later you give me heart attack, then how? His back bends like a broken hanger. *You should lock it away*, he says to its handler. This one is house dog.

It's his age and gait, the other owners tell me. Most of them are decent and have stopped coming, but Bailey and I learn to be there for him. She's a black mongrel with three good legs—a rescue from much worse. The week she gets sick he stays on the pavement, eyeing me through the leaves. Another time when he's yelling, she pads up and licks an open toe, and his face starts to tremble. I should call the police, he says, apoplectic. This one is house dog.

The girl with the German Shepherd finds where he lives and sets all his small birds free. *They were miserable and caged*, she confides and I nod, as if misery was something that simply found its way in. That night at the park he is irresistible, swinging a large bag of trash. Bailey bursts from my grip and returns with it proudly. When I get down to search, he begins to plead. Inside there is nothing - no collar, no leash. The only rings are the ones from beer cans, and a thin brown liquid pools like pee. *This one is house dog*, he whimpers, *what else can I do?* He looks at me like a distant image. Then in November the air changes, and he stops coming, and we walk past his white funeral. (300 words)

Alastair Wee is a writer from Singapore who writes short speculative fiction.

Dark Alley
Ong Chao Hong

Ong Chao Hong is a cartoonist, children's book illustrator, video producer and media educator. He is also a stay-at-home dad who loves to cook, read and strum the ukulele. You can see his cartoons on Instagram @doodlesinabox.

Inspired
Alaka Rajan Skinner

She looked out her bedroom window at the bloodstained setting sun, the arresting palette that never looked the same from one day to the next. *Like a fingerprint, never duplicated.*

She considered herself as an artist, and her greatest source of inspiration was nature, even though she knew she could never truly replicate the wonder that was the natural world. It was criminal that so much of this world on this tiny island-state, which had little room to spare, was sacrificed at the altar of progress. But she was grateful for the kaleidoscopic oasis of her garden, its azure hydrangea, milky frangipani and tangerine birds of paradise. The mango tree beyond the gate, too, was an endless source of pleasure. Like its perennially flowering counterparts peppered across the island, it was flush with foliage and fruit, attracting striking golden orioles that worked in pairs. Partners-in-crime. Oh, how she wished that she had a partner...

She turned back to her bedroom. A pity about the carpet, but at least it was not the expensive Persian carpet in the living room downstairs. The blood spatter from the blow had created fascinating abstract patterns all over it. The blond hair, once beautiful, was now caked with blood in parts, making it a little less attractive than she had envisioned. Still, the hues were mesmerising: the golden tresses, the splashes of crimson and then the rich emerald of the carpet, a stunning background, that perfect counterpoint.

A smiled played upon her lips. Yes, she was an artist, and nature had always been her greatest source of inspiration. (263 words)

Dr Alaka Rajan Skinner is storyteller and executive coach with a PhD (NTU), an MBA (Cornell) and a Masters (Rutgers). She's lived in Iran, India, the US, and now, Singapore. Her book, *Are You Listening?* was on BBC radio, the Singapore Eco Film Festival, the Asian Festival of Children's Content.

A Ravaged Body
James Tan

James Tan is an illustrator, art educator and comic artist. He likes to draw quirky stuff and is known for his "studied carelessness" style. He gets his inspirations while watching people and stirring his kopi siew dai at the kopitiam. Find him on Instagram as @cktanjames.

Dying To See
Moses Sia

Why interview me? Afterall, I am just one painting in this huge gallery. Yes, a picture speaks a thousand words, but I will keep this brief. Never know when words will be needed again.

You could say that I am a relatively popular painting and quite easy on the eye. The young ones catch a glimpse of a not-too-distant past when hawkers ply the streets, the older folks get their jolt of reminiscing and tourists see in me a contrast to the orderly and sanitised streets of today.

Everyone has viewed me with mild curiosity except that wizened old man. I studied this *ah pek* closely, as you would a fascinating artwork, and I could see faded traces of tattoos on his wrinkled tanned skin.

When *ah pek* was pushed into the gallery in his wheelchair, he immediately remarked that it was all too dark for him. Still, he was on an important mission to find this painting he saw on television. Glaucoma was stealing his vision, and this was his precious last chance. At each painting, he strained to see, shook his head vigorously before asking to move to the next.

At last, he found me. The tears in his eyes did not help him see. Strangely, *ah pek* was transfixed by my painting's background at my top right corner, your left. He struggled to stand, his companion helped.

"Me," he gestured like the figure he was pointing at. "Last time, I gangster. Gave *teh gu* money, still they come." He became livid. "This snake even worse," he jabbed in the air at the figure beside. "Bloody sold me out!" He swore and quite unexpectedly, passed out. With that, his uniformed companion quickly wheeled him away.

And yes, that's my statement, officer. (293 words)

Moses Sia is an educator-artist who delights in exploring creativity both personally and in helping others to do the same. He practises as a community artist, especially among seniors, and often uses a blend of traditional and digital media. Moses has illustrated and written picture books and interactive educational games.

Albularyo
Jeff David

Inside his barong-barong, the faith healer poured plenty of water over the man's feet resting in the basin. The water began to blur as he washed away the dirt.

"You must confess all of your sins," he stood and stepped back. "I can pray for your soul, but I can't save it." The people witnessing the act applauded and were amazed by his words.

He made his way to many sick patients. The blind, the deaf, the lame and crippled, even those with cancer. Some travelled from distant towns to the *albularyo*, unsatisfied with their doctor's diagnosis.

He took the hand of a girl—she spoke gibberish and had seizures. "Epilepsy," said the crying mother. "An evil entity is possessing her!" The mother wailed as foam bubbled up in her daughter's mouth.

"I will heal her. Don't interfere," said the man. He raised his right hand and said a prayer. The girl fought back, and began to convulse on the ground. He shouted her name, slapped her cheeks, and made her confess the entity's name. Everyone gasped at the eerie violence akin to a horror film, but to those who needed help, it didn't matter.

People were healed by his faith anyway, and some swore they saw his powers as though he were Jesus himself. No one believed there were consequences. It did not matter. A simple donation was a small sacrifice for those afflicted.

"Your acting is so believable. Here's your thirty percent, as usual. We need to work harder or people will stop coming," he said. He shut the door, went to the window, and gazed into the dark at a building's silhouette. A private hospital stood still. (280 words)

Jeff David is currently taking BA Language and Literature programme at the University of the Philippines Baguio. Born and raised in a small town in Tarlac, David mostly writes about the unique and complex provincial life with references to religion.

Strong
Claire Betita de Guzman

They took turns choosing their next victim. In Manila Bay, it was easy: the sunset was spectacular, and the coconut trees swayed with the breeze, so the vibe was open, carefree. Carmen had never read a guidebook in her life, but she'd concluded Manila Bay must be top of the list, because all tourists went there.

She always chose the men—the stronger and sturdier they looked, the better. "Why these giants?" Uncle Anton often complained. He'd make a show of rubbing muscle balm on his shoulders, twisted and aching, he'd say, from dragging a drugged man from restaurant to taxi.

Secretly, Carmen was always afraid that a woman wouldn't be able to take it. She knew what Ativan, in unchecked doses, could do. She herself shuddered at the effects: the dizziness and palpitations. The wooziness. The long, deep black-out. The men with muscles and heft, they were the ones who could survive this drug's silent attack.

So, she always chose someone who looked strong. She already knew, working this trade for years, that physical strength didn't mean that they weren't unhappy, discontented, or weak. It didn't mean they weren't lonely.

These strong men, they said yes on the first try. Perhaps, they felt brave. Or liked the idea of living on the edge. Perhaps they felt they were equipped with enough brawn and wit to save themselves, should things get awry.

But how could things go wrong when it's just an old couple and their daughter who befriends them? Who needed saving from just another provincial lass like Carmen, who just wants to take selfies with her phone?

These questions become meaningless the moment these men, once ramrod and strong, turn limp and unconscious—all because they couldn't say no to a family's friendly invitation to eat and drink. (300 words)

Claire Betita de Guzman is a former editor at *Cosmopolitan Philippines* and *Harper's Bazaar Singapore*. She is author of the novels, *Miss Makeover, Budget is the New Black, Girl Meets World*, and *No Boyfriend Since Birth*, (adapted for TV). Her latest, *Sudden Superstar*, is forthcoming from Penguin Random House SEA.

The Musician
Chinie Hidalgo Diaz

He lay still and silent, starved for breath, in his final days. She paid no heed to the nurses' clucks and sympathetic sighs. Every day she would sit by his side and clasp his hand. Glare at the machine that measured the oxygen in his blood. And sing.

Moon River.
Beyond the Sea.
Time After Time.
When I Fall in Love.

All the classics he adored.

He was a singer. A songwriter. A musician. Not in the real world, no. He was too straitlaced and pragmatic for that. But where it mattered, he was a musician.

At home, playing the piano, singing second voice as he taught the kids a melody. In the hearty choruses of every family gathering. In his hometown under the coconut trees, strumming a five-string guitar with his drunken chums. He was a musician.

So, in that stark, sterile room, because his beleaguered lungs wouldn't let him be the thing he loved most, she took his hand and his place – and she sang.

As he listened, lying very still, the numbers on his oxygen machine would start to rise.

"90! 91!" she'd point, elated.

"It's not a karaoke machine," her sister smirked.

"93! 95!" she crowed and sang some more.

Her songs didn't save him. Nobody could. But she liked to think they breathed a little bit of life into his blood. And on the days she felt his loss, like a melancholy tune tugging at her heart, it mattered. (244 words)

Chinie Hidalgo Diaz is a copywriter, content strategist and corporate trainer based in Metro Manila. In her downtime, she enjoys beach days, food quests, poetry and the pursuit of the perfect cookie.

Never the Flesh Forever
Danny Jalil

Danny Jalil wrote the comics *Lt. Adnan and the Last Regiment*, and *Elizabeth Choy: Her Story*. He has spoken at the Singapore Writers Festival and the Asian Festival of Children's Content, and conducts writing workshops with SingLit Station. His latest novel, *Enrique the Black*, is out now. Connect with him on Instagram: @dannyjalil_writer

My Everything
Rizza Corella Punsalan

Work orders me pizza after hours crushed under his weight, screaming as he tears me apart. The pizza is hand-tossed, has no pineapples, and is topped with Angus beef. He knows just how I like it. We eat together in the kitchen, and I try to ignore my reflection in the glass window, the black lines beneath my eyes.

Work encourages my love for alcohol. He drives me to Laslow's nearly every night, hoots and claps as I down shot glass after shot glass, obliterating the yells, the dirty clothes in the hamper, the dishes in the sink. He drives me home, lays me down in bed, and I black out. Whatever else he does, I do not know.

Work pushes me to be the best I can be. He encourages me to write S.M.A.R.T. goals, pulls me a little too hard out of the couch, hides my phone in his safe, makes sure I follow my cleaning schedule. *I just want you to live up to your full potential,* he says. *I want you to say that I make you a better person.*

Work constantly messages me when he's stuck at the office, makes sure I'm well. When I admit I'm sad, he thinks I'm being pessimistic. When I don't reply, he calls me up and concludes something is wrong and I'm not telling him what it is. I say everything is fine. He asks me about my curt replies, accuses me of putting an embarrassingly small amount of effort into our relationship. I hang up. I try to sleep.

I call my mother, tell her I'm going to end it. She objects, saying he's good for me, he takes care of me. And what would I really be without him? (292 words)

Rizza Corella Punsalan is an MA Creative Writing student at the University of the Philippines Diliman. She writes code to make a living, but writes words and music to feel alive. Her works have been published in *Five Minutes*, *Dark Winter Lit*, and *Short Fiction Break*.

The Price of Belief
Victor Fernando R. Ocampo

The glow of four ambient laser-diode screens grows bright enough to stir you from your sleep. You are lying in bed, rubbing some gunk from the corner of your left eye. Your right eye is idle, so you task it with searching for your HDB-approved holographic dog. You spy him idling at his charging dock.

Eye gunk removed, you look around with both eyes. The rental one-room flat you're in is small and hexagonal, like the cell of a beehive. Apart from the bed, there is only a built-in counter for cooking and eating, a small bookshelf, and a long work desk.

There is an annoying reminder blinking on one of the ambient screens. It warns you that a loan you took is critically near default. You bin the message as soon as you read it.

"I have to go to work," you tell your holographic dog.

You dress for success and head towards your job supervising maintenance robots at Raffles Place. Unfortunately, your industry-competitive paycheque isn't enough to cover your bills, your mother's mounting medical expenses, and pay off the loan you needed to get to this land of mythical plenty.

You cling to your dreams but belief is expensive. On the MRT ride, you feel dark thoughts welling up inside you—do you really need both your kidneys? So what if you sold one lung, or your unique heartbeat pattern? Ovaries? You never really wanted kids anyway.

Outside, the rain falls in thick sheets. Rivulets of grey water quickly obscure the city from your view. You don't know whether to cry or scream, because you left your umbrella at the flat of the meaningless fuck you had the other night.

The MRT dives underground and you shut your eyes tight. (276 words)

Victor Fernando R. Ocampo is the author of the International Rubery Book Award shortlisted *The Infinite Library and Other Stories* (Math Paper Press, 2017, US edition; Gaudy Boy, 2021) and *Here be Dragons* (Canvas Press, 2015), which won the Romeo Forbes Children's Story Award in 2012.

Underground Identity
Ho See Kum

Ho See Kum is an established art educator with 20 years of teaching experience in the industry. He is an artist, art educator and content creator for ComixGuru's LearnXArt programme for school art and enrichment classes. He has conducted cartooning workshops at Nanyang Academy of Fine Arts and taught at Gradsign Art School between 2003 – 2007.

I Have a Secret!
Glenn Russel D. Alejon

I'm stuck. The closet became smaller, but the house became bigger. What should I do? (15 words)

Glenn Russel D. Alejon is a sophomore in the University of the Philippines Diliman. His interest is piqued by topics revolving around queer experience for gender equality and justice.

Orange
Z.L. Mercado

"It's been three months," I told the nurse who was interviewing me.

He nodded and began to scribble away "And do you think the meds are helping?"

Were they helping? I ask myself.

I feel drowsier throughout the day. I've been getting fatter, even with the extra effort to go to the gym. And meds aren't cheap. But in return, I can get out of bed instead of wallowing in it all day. I can complete more tasks and talk to people with less fear. I can go outside without sweating.

"Yes, I think they are," I replied.

"And how do you feel right now? Are you elated, depressed... somewhere in between?"

I didn't even know that I was depressed. Not until my doctor diagnosed me. Depression is funny like that. It creeps into your mind and stays there unknowingly. It's not blue the way people describe it, nor is it purple or green with cool, soothing undertones. It's definitely not a bright and sunny yellow.

Depression is orange. An awkward, fickle, uncomfortable orange. Sometimes it feels natural, like carrots, and *kwek-kwek*, and a fat, grumpy cat. But sometimes it's annoying, like the ray of sunlight piercing through your eyelids as you try to sleep throughout the day because you don't have the motivation to do anything.

"I feel... in between." I answered. I'm not going to tell the nurse I feel orange. The rest of the consultation was uneventful. I continued to live my orange-coloured life. Sometimes it pairs with blue creating a disgusting combination. But sometimes it's mixed with yellow, a great pairing that can lift any spirits. (270 words)

Z.L Mercado is a student of language and literature in the Philippines. His interest lies in observing and portraying the human psyche and experience from a new perspective. Writing also gives him the opportunity to be artistically vulnerable which he takes pride in.

Three
Jenny Faith Koh

Joy stops in her tracks.

Did I turn off all the lights and switches? I've checked three times. I'll be late for work if I go back now.

"Three" is the number of times Joy and her therapist agreed that Joy would do these checks.

A voice intrudes into her mind.

If you don't turn off the lights, you waste money. If the wires overheat and they catch fire, you burn the whole house down. Make sure you double lock the door or else robbers …

Joy runs back to her block.

She turns the key in the door lock twice and walks around the house. Her eyes sweep over every switch.

"Off." She says aloud for every turned-off switch she sees in case she needs to recall this scene later.

Perspiration drips down her back. Her throat parched. She inspects the windows. "Locked, locked."

She leaves her house and turns the key twice. *Or else.*

In the lift, she looks at her phone.

Late again. I failed again. I gave in to my illness. Why couldn't I stop at three?

The lift doors reopen to a woman with permed hair and a shopping trolley of groceries. "Late for work again? Did you switch off everything?"

"I told you to stop asking me these questions. You need to seek professional help."

"You also stop. I already told you I'm not siao. The monthly allowance, can give more? Remember, we raise you until so big and educated, okay. Hello! I'm talking to you. You walk away? Pretend didn't hear, is it?"

Joy sits at the bus stop. She stares at the moving traffic, considering that one step could end it all.

Her phone beeps with a reminder, "Therapy, 7:00 pm."

"At least, not today then." (294 words)

Jenny Faith Koh is a writer and mental health advocate from Singapore. She writes stories to give voice to the overlooked and unheard. Her stories have appeared at the Singapore Writers Festival, *The Lumiere Review*, and elsewhere. She is the co-founder of a mental health podcast *I Feel Fine Really*.

Anxiety
Anngee Neo

Anngee Neo is a Singapore-based illustrator who creates drawings with an emphasis on storytelling with compelling characters. Her quirky, surreal and whimsical works have breathed life to children's books such as *The Rock and the Bird* and *Do Gallery Sitters Sit All Day? Things People Really Do In A Museum*. She has made illustrations for campaigns and books for clients such as National Gallery Singapore, National Museum of Singapore and Esplanade.

If Travis Bickle had been a Singaporean
Francis Lau

He sticks a joint in the corner of his mouth, tries to light it but the match he's holding won't strike. Could be the wind that's blowing in his face, causing the joint to somehow slip out. He bends forward to pick it up from the ground. He strikes another match. Finally, he lights up, takes a drag, then rises from his seat. As he paces the floor, his skinny gait waxes like two pistons in locomotion. He has an agenda to fulfil, yet he doesn't seem to know where, or how, or why. He continues to maunder, to and fro, from the stalls at the coffeeshop and back to his table. Soon he picks a particular stall, and tries to chat a young girl up. A pixie with fabulous body art. But she turns a blind eye, and he realises how much she's like the rest—cold and distant. As he slinks away, all of a sudden, he remembers his beer is growing old. He whispers to himself, steadies a drinking straw and sips from his pint with a smile. (182 words)

Francis Lau writes occasionally to de-stress. Less is more is a deceptively simple truth that he tries to live out every day.

Otterly Gorgeous
Danielle Lim

The two otters splash in the rolling water as the breeze carries their squeaks into the warm sunlight. They must catch the sun while they can, while there's still two of them, the young man thinks, as he leans on his knees, panting from the solo run.

His name was Oliver. They called him Ollie. Not this young man, but the one he used to run with.

The last time he saw Ollie was a month ago. They were jogging in Bishan Park when they saw the otters frolicking in the water. With eyes, he now recalls, that were glazed with the sheen of desperate hope, Ollie said they were otterly gorgeous.

No, the last time he saw Ollie was not a month ago. It was yesterday as Ollie lay in the coffin. Wait, wasn't it just yesterday, they were running together, catching the sun? Everything is mixed up. When the last time was. He and his buddy. The sweat and the tears on their faces.

Ollie jumped.

If he had known, could he have done something, said something, to change life's trajectory? Perhaps confused people ask questions which are impossible to answer, not so much a question as it is an anguished expression of regret.

The two otters begin swimming away. *Goodbye Ollie*, he chokes. *Did you want to tell us that if you kept running, the world couldn't tell your sweat from your tears, and everyone would still think that your life was gorgeous?* (276 words)

Danielle Lim is an award-winning author whose books have won the Singapore Book Awards 2021 and the Singapore Literature Prize 2016. Her work has been translated and published in Taiwan and India. Her latest novel, *All Our Brave, Earthly Scars*, was published by Penguin Random House SEA in 2022.

Computer Hang
Don Low

Don Low graduated with a Master in Animation from Savannah College of Art & Design in Georgia, USA, and is currently teaching in a local university. Don's passion is drawing and sketching as much as time allows him to do so. His works are featured in *The Art of Urban Sketching, An Illustrated Life Vol.2, Urban Sketchers Singapore Vol 1*, and *Urban Sketching: The Complete Guide to Techniques* and *Liquid City 2*. He published his second graphic novel, *Kungfu Dough*, in 2018.

Jump
Janet Hui Ching Tay

The scream. Then wailing, shaking. Strangers, shocked, horrified, surround her. Someone calls the police. Cover it up. Blood seeps into the pebbled Japanese garden where he'd landed. Call the cleaners. The crying never ceases. Murmurs. Low voices, averted glances, but the wife notices nothing except pain.

A call to school is made. A child summoned. Puzzled. Told nothing, asked to wait until he sees his mother. A kind teacher drives him to the apartment building. Police everywhere, he's so curious. Exciting. Then he sees his mother, broken, hysterical, like she isn't anyone he knows. He looks at the police officer who smiles at him pityingly. He's only eight but he already knows.

So, he thinks of flying kites and days at the beach. Ice-cream cones and surprise toys from business travels. Their favourite restaurant. Hide and seek. Piggyback rides and wrestling matches. Long drives to nowhere. Learning to ride the bicycle. A nod, a smile, a pat on the back. Good job.

His mother takes his hand, and they sit on a bench. She hugs him, the tears won't stop. He hears mostly echoes. He already feels emptier. His school bag on his back. He's still holding his water bottle. The officer comes and tells his mother the ambulance will pick up the body. She weeps and holds him tighter. He can feel her hot tears wetting the sleeves of his uniform. He tries to breathe in her scent, but there is no perfume today, only the stench of nothingness.

Another one, the neighbours whisper. It was a teenager two months ago. How awful. Maybe work stress. Depression. Hope nobody knows, trying to rent out my unit. Shhh. Here she comes. Poor boy. They seemed like a happy family. Who knew. (291 words)

Janet Hui Ching Tay's short stories have appeared in various anthologies. The first act of her full-length play, *Reunion*, was longlisted for the 2017 Windsor Fringe Kenneth Branagh Award for New Drama Writing. She is a Tin House Winter Workshop 2023 alum and lives in Kuala Lumpur with her husband and her son.

If I Die
Rajendiran Suresh

It will be easier for you if I die, Bhee. I can't see you this way, Bhee. You won't cry over my death, you just have to turn on another light. I'm sure you won't lose.

I'm nothing, Bhee. To see you drown in anguish makes my soul weaker, and my body is tired. It's getting dim.

I'm going to leave you soon. Extinguish all my flames. Death can't be denied. And actually, I'm not afraid of my death. I'm just afraid to be apart from you.

I won't see your face again. I'm afraid to miss you. I'm afraid if I die, you will be dissolved in even more darkness. But my last fear is unfounded.

You have a lot of light around you. You will easily find a replacement for me.

If I die, later, all you have to do is turn on another light and throw me in the trash bin.

I'm dying. The light of my life is only a faint flicker. I know my time won't be long. My prayer is only one. "Lord, when I go, don't let her get lost in the dark."

With your own eyes, you watched me die. For the last time I whispered in your ear. You can't lose. You just have to find a new light and come out of your darkness.

Goodbye, Bhee. I'm off forever. But I'm sure that once I die, you won't lose. You will easily replace my corpse with a new, brighter lightbulb. And I'm not sorry, because I know. I've been there, hanging from the roof of your house, pulling you out of the dark. (273 words)

Rajendiran Suresh hails from Cuddalore, a district in Tamil Nadu, India. He is a migrant worker and has been working in Singapore in the construction section for almost nine years. He likes to do photography, video editing, and writing occasionally in his free time.

Christmas Mourn
Chris Ramos

It was not the rooster's crowing that roused six-year-old cousins Chloe and Colleen out of slumber. Neither was it the scuffling of "Santa" clumsily slipping out of the sheets to carelessly stuff their stockings with stickers and stationery. Nor was it the jingling of the chapel bells next door to ring in the birth of Jesus. It wasn't the cacophony of Christmas karaoke either.

The sound was unlike an alarm; it wasn't rhythmic, reverberating, riotous, or redundant. Instead, it was slow and sticky, warm and raw, vibrant and viscous. The sound was guttural, it had gravitas, there was grief. At first, the sound was crimson in colour, then it deepened into burgundy, and finally settled into rust, staining their minds with this memory, that moment they realised what it was that woke them up.

It was the sound of a sacrificial pig being slaughtered for the sake of a Christmas celebration— to be skewered and spun on a stick, roasted over fire for over five hours, until it was radiant and red, and then laid to rest on a bed of banana leaves with an apple in its mouth, to be skinned and dipped into liver sauce later on by the very same kids who, just that morning, vowed never to eat pork again, because they felt sorry for the pig they had played with and petted just the day before. (231 words)

Chris Ramos is a Jill of a few trades, but a master of none, and that's okay. She's a self-taught artist, a pandemic writer, a YouTube piano student, a yoga teacher, an explorer, a former dancer, a full-time feminist, and a furrent to her criminal cats, Felony, Larceny, and Perjury.

Draconian
Judy Tham

Uncle Choo said I would die tomorrow.

That's what everyone here calls him—Uncle Choo, with his perfectly-ironed Dacron blue uniform and shiny buckle. He prefers that to Warden Choo.

I'm scared. Of course, I'm scared. I don't know what I've done to deserve this.

Death.

After all, I was just following my boss's order. Mummy always tells me to do whatever boss says, or I'll lose my job. And I always did. Even though he made me fight with other guys and collect debts for him. It hurt when I got injured from the fights, but I never complained.

How did I end up here? Boss told me to bring back some coke from Thailand to Singapore. What's wrong with that? I mean, we drink coke all the time, don't we? I asked him why the coke was in powder form, not in bottles. He laughed and said nothing. Then he taped several packets on my inner thigh near my *kukubird*. They should be safe because no one would go near my *kukubird*, he said. But the police at Changi Airport searched me and found them. And boy, were they mad! They pinned me down on the floor and locked me here for many years.

When I stood before the judge in court, the lawyers said my IQ was only 62 and that I was intellectually challenged and possibly mentally disabled. But 62 is good, right? I remember the teacher in school said I'd pass if I scored 50 or more marks, although I seldom did.

Apparently, I wasn't mentally disabled, although I still don't know what it means.

Mummy will be sad if I die. But can someone please explain to me, why do I have to die? (290 words)

Judy Tham was born in Singapore and obtained her bachelor degree from the National University of Singapore. She is the author of the novel *My American Sister* and co-author of *Are You Brand Dead?*, a book on branding. She lives in Singapore, where she also lectures at higher learning institutions.

Answer the Question
Daniel Seifert

Then one day you see a strange man hunched behind a table. Maybe you've left work after a punishing day you've already forgotten. Maybe, blinking as a dying sunset winks gold into your eyes, you almost walk past the cheap picnic table and its faded sign.

"THE SCARIEST QUESTION YOU'LL EVER BE ASKED. $130," it says. The man is aged between 47 and 74. His face is lined and oaken, impassive but smiling. You can't tell if his creased eyes look your way.

You open your mouth but your partner rings. The baby's coming. You trot to a bus to stand on the bus to ignore other passengers, tired from their work and trotting to the bus to ignore you to get home. You forget about the man.

Then one day you see him again.

You are at your kid's football game, not watching the youthful chaos, wondering what time you can be somewhere else. At the edge of the field, dying leaves caked around the table legs, you see the sign. "THE SCARIEST QUESTION YOU'LL EVER BE ASKED. $1,300." The man waves at you — you think he's waving at you — you wonder why you wish he wasn't.

You take your child home and try not to think about the man. Your kid asks if you saw their goal. I sure did, you lie.

You see the man, off and on, every time you forget about him. You age, he doesn't. The sign remains the same, the price goes up, up.

Then one day, you're aged between 47 and 74, you thrust him needy stacks of bills, you say, *Tell me the question*. He smiles.

Slides over a piece of paper and you open it with lined and oaken hands, and read three words, no question mark:

Are you happy.

(300 words)

After 12 years as a marketing exec, Daniel Seifert is taking a sabbatical to try his hand at fiction. Currently a Masters student at LASALLE College of the Arts, he hopes to one day publish a novel or, failing that, invent a time machine and invest in Bitcoin back in 2009.

Into The Light

Therese Jamora-Garceau

Peng woke up and found himself in a gauzy, new world. It looked like his bedroom, but everything was blurred around the edges. There was a pool of vomit at the foot of his bed. Eww, gross. Gotta clean that up. He went to get a mop from Nita in the kitchen, but no matter how loud he shouted, she didn't seem to see or hear him. He tried tapping her on the shoulder, and his hand went through, as if she were ectoplasm. He hurried back to his room and—how could he have missed it the first time?—saw his body splayed near the vomit, a baggie of pills close by.

Oh, my God, I'm dead!

"Yeah, you're dead," echoed a bored voice.

Peng looked up and saw a young man who looked remarkably like his cousin Nico, who died in a car accident years ago.

"At least you died like a rock star," Nico said. "I mean, who chokes on their own vomit these days?"

"I can't be dead," Peng insisted. "There are so many things I haven't done; so many things I haven't finished!"

"Well, too late now, cuz," Nico drawled. "At least you got forty days to get your affairs in order."

"Forty days?" Peng squeaked. "And then what?"

"And then... you go into the light. Or not. I hear it's awesome, though."

"Then why haven't you gone?"

"I still got things to do. Never told this girl I loved her, for one. Been trying to find a way to do that."

"Good luck with that, bro."

"Good luck to you, too, Peng. This place isn't too different from before. Same problems, same unresolved shit. But I hope to see you *there* soon!" (288 words)

Therese Jamora-Garceau is a writer and editor who's written short stories for both *Fast Food Fiction* and *Fast Food Fiction Delivery*. She's also the drummer for alt-pop band The Garceaus, who are releasing five new songs on Spotify to complete their debut album, *Beautiful Mistake*.

Room for One
Selene Estaris

Hey, welcome! We're so glad you made it. Let me escort you to where you'll be staying.

Right here, the door on the left. This is your place.

Please, come in and make yourself at home. We've fit it to your preferences and really hope you like it.

We've heard from a couple of your friends that you liked warm, earthy tones and a cosy atmosphere, so we tried to integrate that here, as you can tell from the furnishings.

Through this door is your personal library. Your mum was quite helpful in selecting the books that we've stocked your shelves with. All your favourite authors are here—we even have copies of books you had back home.

Right through this sliding door is your listening room and cinema. Your dad and siblings are personally responsible for this one.

Vinyl, cassettes, CDs.

Turntables, stereo system, headphones.

All the music and film your heart could desire.

Over here, you'll find your kitchen, where we've prepared some welcome meals. Your grandparents gushed about how much you loved these dishes—a couple of which are their specialties, I believe.

Lastly, out here is a small garden where you might recognise those little friends frolicking in the grass over there.

Now, before I leave, I have a favour to ask. Whenever you're ready, I'd love to hear about the rest of the people in your life. Anything you can remember. It will really help us better accommodate them when it's time.

As for those who are already here, they can't wait to see you again.

Anyway, I best be on my way. I have a couple more appointments at the front desk. If you ever need anything, just ring and ask for Peter. (289 words)

Selene Estaris is an aspiring writer from the Philippines. Currently, she works as a grade school teacher who occasionally squeezes in time to weave short stories inspired by the world around her. A lover of horror, her works usually revolve around darker themes but every now and then, they venture beyond.

Hermit GPT
Cheah Sinann

Cheah Sinann is a former editorial cartoonist with *The Straits Times*, where he also produced the popular comic strip *The House of Lim*. His present cartoon strip, *Budi & Saltie*, which highlights environmental issues, appears in *The Borneo Bulletin* in Brunei. Cheah has also published two graphic novels, *The Bicycle* (2014) and *Terumbu* (2018).

Storefronts
Michaela Benedicto

When it was all over, we came out of hiding, but none of the places we knew are there. There had been a reshuffling: the café at the corner now sells scientific equipment; the bar with the cork walls have completely disappeared. People spill out of storefronts, re-reading the signs.

We can no longer navigate our own city. The streets are unrecognisable, and there is no use remembering. The young sit on the sidewalk watching the old folks go by, searching for the right address.

"There's a party tonight," says one. "I wonder who'll be there." (96 words)

Micaela Benedicto was born in 1977 and works as an architect, artist and musician in Manila. She runs her own design practice and is part of the dreampop duo Outerhope. Her visual art has been exhibited in several galleries and lies in the intersection of photography and sculpture.

Visiting
Zed Yeo

Lao Chen walked along the Clementi canal, down the darkness of Avenue Seven. A rustle from the shrubs. A trickle from the stream. A chill draft from nowhere.

"Leave me alone. I'm just walking home," he said.

She murmured. The air shifted.

"Leave me alone."

She grinned. *This is not your lane.*

"I want to see my grandson. He is calling. Today is the last day."

Go through the forest. This is not your lane.

"What d'you want? I'm in a hurry. Food? I can give you my chicken rice."

More.

"Fine. My watch? Freshy burnt. Rolex. I'll give you 100 million as well."

More.

"Hmm. What else?"

Teacup.

"Bu ke yi."

I want… teacup.

"Bu. Ke. Yi. You are asking for too much. Negotiation's over," Lao Chen grumbled. He walked on in her direction. As he passed her, she showed teeth, her pale neck snaked through the dark, and her head dangled over Chen's shoulder. Mischief and murder brightened her face.

A head rolled on the rough tarmac.

In a dusty flat, there was a wooden altar, and a tablet. A boy had prayed to a tablet till he had unwittingly fallen asleep. The plate of chicken rice in front of the altar, was meant to be eaten hot. Lao Chen was too late for that.

It was rainy and windy, but for a moment, the room warmed up. The boy smiled in his sleep.

Lao Chen sniffed the XO in a teacup beside the chicken rice. His favourite.

"Gong, come earlier next time," said the boy in his sleep. Kids are sensitive. They can sense. "But don't bring strange things into the house next year kay' Gong?" the boy added.

Lao Chen looked at the head in his hand. Then he sipped his XO. "Okay," he quipped. (299 words)

Zed Yeo has authored over 10 books, including *Half Ghost* and multiple works in the *Saurus* Series. A recipient of the National Arts Council's Presentation and Participation Grant, Zed has been a speaker at events such as the Asian Festival of Children's Content and Young Writers Festival.

In an Instance
Veronica Leow

Veronica Leow is a Singapore-based digital illustrator and animator. A self-taught artist, Veronica first realised her passion for illustration when she began digital drawing on her phone. As of 2021, she has upgraded her illustration skills (and software!) in her studies at LASALLE College of the Arts.

Screaming Woman
Loh Guan Liang

When the residents of Admiralty found dead bees littering their streets, they blamed it on the weather. Everyone went on with their lives. No one thought it was a problem. Not until dumbbells started cratering roofs and shattering windscreens in other parts of Singapore.

The police were alerted. Some pressed their Town Councils for answers. Others wanted compensation. There was none. In response, a bag of toilet plungers appeared outside a police post in Bedok with a sign declaring, GIVE ME BACK MY SKY.

Prodded into action by fish balls pelting government buildings, the Prime Minister's Office announced a state of emergency. "We must work together as One Singapore," the Prime Minister said, "under shelter." But what can a talking head of state on a screen do? No amount of diplomacy or taxes could deflect the threat of death from above! Even the air force, coast guard and checkpoint authorities were helpless against this siege of foreign bodies invading our shores.

Students studied from home. Employees worked from home. Parents parented from home—or at least, everyone tried to. The food delivery industry collapsed under a nation's boredom and hunger.

Yesterday, heavy clouds massed over Marina Bay.

Today, a woman fell from the sky screaming. (205 words)

Loh Guan Liang is the author of two poetry collections: *Transparent Strangers* and *Bitter Punch*. *Bitter Punch* was shortlisted for the Singapore Literature Prize in 2018. In 2014, he co-translated *Art Studio*, a Chinese novel by Singapore Cultural Medallion recipient Yeng Pway Ngon. Guan Liang updates at http://lohguanliang.weebly.com

Acceptance
Paul Eric Roca

Paul Eric Roca is a freelance artist from the Philippines. He is a painter, children's book illustrator, and an editorial cartoonist. He worked for Adarna House as an in-house artist, as an editorial illustrator for *The Straits Times* of Singapore, and an editorial cartoonist for *The Manila Bulletin*. Currently, he is a member of cartooning groups; Pitik Bulag (Philippines), The Cartoon Movement (the Netherlands), and Cartooning for Peace (France).

Messages
Rosanna Licari

Fire, plague and then flood. 10,000 people displaced. No wonder the Jehovah Witnesses are sending me unsolicited mail with biblical references. Reaching out "to share something positive" —a quote from Luke (21:5)—*Look! I make all things new*. I'm in the middle of several fractured plots. There are bodies in fridges and water. Binge-viewing "crime" has distorted narratives, as I try to remember which episode belongs to which TV series. And in two different series, the detective is the same actor. My friend lost the contents of her home. Walls swell and smell in the body of the house. The two arms of the Wilsons River overflowed. Lismore became a lake. Dwellings untouched in 1974 didn't escape. Not enough SES equipment or anything else. Kayaks drifted between the roofs where people waited. My friend saw her heavy wooden table and chairs rise and float freely in the dining room. A watery seance. She swam out. Luke the Evangelist hooked in more followers for the Son of God. Gave a history from birth to ascension. But resurrection seems impossible for the politicians on TV. Their fingerprints are all over the place. My friend measured each ballot paper against that waterline. (199 words)

Rosanna Licari has an Istrian-Italian background. Her poetry collection *An Absence of Saints* (UQP) won the Thomas Shapcott Manuscript Prize, the Anne Elder Poetry Award, and the Wesley Michel Wright Award. Her latest collection *Earlier* (Ginninderra Press) was published in 2023. She is the poetry editor of *StylusLit* at www.styluslit.com.

P(X)
Dennis Yeo

6:26. He had timed it perfectly. The odds were staggering; and therein lay the anticipation. He had played this game of trial and error many times, never getting it right. In life, as with Science, there were constants and variables, but life was not a controlled environment. The universe orbited around chance, was ruled by fate and was subject to serendipity. A minute more or less could make all the difference. 6:26 was the only constant he could control.

Snooze. Air-con. Blanket. Snuggle. Alarm. Groan.

His haversack sat beside him. He had positioned himself strategically, a measured distance from the entrance. His senses were heightened. He remembered the first time he had seen her with her friends, in her white and blue uniform. She wasn't particularly striking. It was the lilt of her laughter, the music in her voice and the sway of her bob. Other times alone, with a book for companion, she questioned Physics, smiled at Neruda or dreamt philosophy.

Ready. Milo. Sip. Pause. Sip. Pause. Text.

She was his muse. What CCA was she in? Any siblings? Dogs or cats? He wondered what music she listened to, what her weekends were like, what shampoo she used. He searched for her each morning, and when his eyes would light on her face, all seemed right with the world.

Lift. Stop. Down. Stop. Down. Open. Green. Cross.

6:28. Did he miss her? Six passengers alighted. Four empty seats. Then three. Two. Now one. He saw her ascend; alone! Two people before her. Last seat gone. The boy in front of her saw someone and walked past him. He removed his haversack.

She looked at the seat, looked at him, then he felt himself momentarily lifted as the weight of her bottom puffed up the seat.

Breathe. (297 words)

When he is not teaching at the National Institute of Education, Singapore, Dennis Yeo lives an alternate reality of music, movies, words, and bubble tea. He has two short stories and some poems published in various anthologies. He believes in serendipity and hopes to bump into Kate Beckinsale one day.

Pick-up
May Tobias-Papa

May Tobias-Papa's day job consists of writing strategic multimedia content for corporations. A visual communications graduate, she also illustrates for children's books, editorials, and websites. May is based in the province of Rizal and is currently pursuing a graduate degree in English Studies at the University of the Philippines.

Manifest
Myrza Sison

It was love at first sight. She knew she wanted to marry him before he had even said a word. She loved his long lashes, his bar-of-soap smell, the way he chewed on the temple tips of his eyeglasses when lost in deep thought. She loved that he loved to read for hours, and that he loved the way she made him coffee. But whenever their eyes met, he was the first to look away. He looked at her, but he never stared. He smiled, but never with teeth. She had many, many photographs of him on her phone, but he did not have a single one of her on his.

The imbalance did not bother her. Anything is possible, she decided. Many long-lasting unions had been built on much less. She could tell he found comfort in her constant presence and attention, and that was enough. Like a flower needs the rain. "I know you need me," she hummed in her head.

She took the liberty of naming their two future children and decided where they would go to school even before such matters could ever occur to him. "You'll thank me later," she thought. Finally, he broke the ice. Her heart soared and then sank a little. She couldn't help but wish that his first words to her were more memorable than "Check, please."

But it didn't matter. Her love would see them through. She knew exactly what to do.

She stared long and hard at the name on his credit card and handed it back to him with a smile. (263 words)

Myrza Sison is a writer, speaker, executive coach, podcaster, content creator, and host. She was the editor-in-chief of Cosmopolitan, Marie Claire, Spot.ph, and Femalenetwork.com. She is also a Palanca Awardee for fiction. Myrza is writing her first collection of short stories and a self-empowerment manual called Join Lang Nang Join.

Dandelion
Tan Ai Qi

She didn't like her hair, not when it was blonde and curled, ready for church on Sunday, not when it was the colour of prunes, limp and tickling her shoulders, not when it was electric blue, falling over her eyes like a lampshade. She didn't like her eyes, brown was the colour of mud, dead leaves and decay. She didn't like her nose, it always lay too flat against her face no matter how much she pinched and scrunched. She didn't like her lips, they were too thin, too pale, too small.

He liked her hair, malleable like clay, morphing to fit her face, its colour changing like traffic lights on the intersection. He liked her eyes, warm and inviting, like hot chocolate on a rainy evening. He liked her nose, the way it moves when she laughs, and how it suddenly appears behind her book, like wild mushrooms after rain. He liked her lips, with its teeth marks like old gum, plump with untold stories.

She looks around at all the roses and lilies, her stout and hairy dandelion body quivering in the wind. She sits in the back, scrunched up like an upside down beetle, hoping no one would notice her struggle. She'd see her face in glass doors, cafeteria cups and car windows and look away. She read stories and put on so many shoes, but none of them fit when it was time to go home.

He looks around at colour—a cacophony, bold, brash and loud, wishing for quiet. He sits beside her, book and mind out of sync, thoughts drifting like pollen. He catches glimpses when she turns, they are fleeting, sacred. He wrote stories for two and made a pair of new shoes, hoping one day he'll show her the way. (298 words)

Tan Ai Qi is currently a Masters in Creative Writing student at LASALLE College of the Arts. She writes both short stories and long-form pieces, and most of her work is fictional. In her spare time, she can be found with a good cup of coffee and her nose in a book.

Breast

Greth Barredo

While showering in the bathroom, she felt with her fingers the stone-like lump in the lower part of her right breast. A few months later, she had the breast surgically removed. The breast was scraped empty. The areola was incised and stitched up. The four-hundred-gram flesh, gone. And its absence made her body feel heavier, not lighter.

One night she dreamed about breast-shaped planets. They orbited her. She floated in space. She couldn't see her own body. She tried to do swimming strokes... she could feel the strain in her muscles... but she remained fixed in her position. As soon as she woke up from the terrible dream, she tugged the collar of her blouse and looked at the clean line of scar on her chest. She began to sob.

She started dating a man six years her junior. She wanted to become a desirable object once and for all. She wanted to feel loved.

One night, he held her against the wall, feeling her up. No. No. Stop. She wanted to protest. The thing inside her blouse was just a ball of foam. She wanted to confess. It wasn't a living material but a tomb. But she let him continue. Suddenly, his eyes went big and rounded as a coin. He quickly withdrew his hand from her body as if he had touched something hot. His face was drained of colour. He stepped away from her. She smiled mockingly at him. She sat on the edge of the bed, crossed her supple legs, watched him as he scrambled to look for his pants. *Bye, honey*, she said. She laughed and blew a kiss, as he reached for the door in his underpants. (283 words)

Greth Barredo is currently working in a media intelligence company that mainly gathers news from Australia and New Zealand. Some of her short stories have appeared in *The Philippines Graphic, Luna Journal PH*, and in several online literary magazines. She lives in the Province of Bulacan with her family.

Auntie Clutter
Quek Hong Shin

Quek Hong Shin is a Singaporean children's book author and illustrator whose works include picture books like *The Amazing Sarong, The Brilliant Oil Lamp*, and *Universe of Feelings*. *The Incredible Basket*, published by Epigram Books, was the winner of Best Children's Book at the 2019 Singapore Book Awards. He hopes to promote the appreciation of local culture with his stories and illustrations.

Liddat Also Can
Clara Mok

"Is she the bride?" old Mr Soo asked, squinting through his thick glasses.

The bride was clad in black T-shirt and denim shorts, showing off her slim legs. Her hair was bunched into a high ponytail in a hotel wedding reception.

"Yes, she is," replied Mdm Lim, clearing her throat.

"Her dressing...?"

"Well, it's her second marriage," she whispered. "That little girl in the pink frock is from her first."

The elderly man shook his head. "*Liddat* also can."

"Look! That boy in a tuxedo," she said, pointing at a four-year-old next to the groom, who was also in black T-shirt and jeans.

"That's the groom's child... with his ex-wife." Mdm Lim paused for effect, then added, "Guess they're even." (119 words)

Clara Mok enjoys the thrill of arranging words into a microfiction and pruning them down. Selected for the Mentor Access Project 2016/17 by National Arts Council, her short stories have been published in *Unsaid anthology, Tapestry of Colours 1 and 2, QLRS* and *Singapore at Home-Life Across Lines*.

Something Wonderful
Dawn Ho

Dawn Ho is a multimedia artist currently residing in Melbourne. Drawing has been a part of her since she was a child. She is also a bossa nova and samba vocalist who has released two albums and is currently recording her third record consisting of her own original songs.

The Rose
Tan Suet Lee

A single red rose lay between her mug and her framed picture of St Peter's Basilica. Grace considered the three mugs on the drying rack in the pantry. Could one of their owners be her admirer? The first belonged to Vincent, an accounts assistant with droopy eyelids who slurred. She smelled his mug. Was that alcohol? The second mug read, "Punch Today in the Face" and belonged to Keong, whose answer to every question was, "Cannot be..." Was he the one? Cannot be. The dark blue one with stains was Mr Tan's. Its colour reminded her of the ocean in winter, though she'd never travelled outside of Singapore.

Mr Tan's wife, Christina, was taller than him, yet still wore heels. Grace knew they were having problems when Mr Tan asked her if she knew of any healthy *tingkat* delivery services. He needed someone to look after him, someone shorter, less vain. With bleach and steel wool, Grace scrubbed his mug till she could see her own reflection. She smiled and made a fresh cup of coffee.

In Mr Tan's office, she was surprised to see him crawling on the floor. "Mr Tan?" Grace asked. "Can I help?"

"I'm missing a rose," he said, overturning files. "It's for Linda in HR... to thank her for—have you seen it?"

Grace thought of her face in the wintery ocean.

"Sorry, I haven't..."

As she peeled the rose petals one by one and flushed them down the toilet, their swirl of red reminded her of blood left from gutted fish. She was glad she had forgotten to rinse out the bleach from his mug. (271 words)

Tan Suet Lee's plays include *Mine (2020), Love in a Time of Covid (2020) and The Swing (2017;2013)*. A published playwright, poet and short story writer, Suet Lee holds a Master of Arts in Creative Writing and is in the final stages of completing her PhD in Creative Writing.

The Hustle
Patrick Sagaram

Ever so often I get recognised when I least expect it. Once I was at this café along Keong Saik Road and I got a DM from a stranger who described what I was wearing. It freaked me out, to be honest. Maybe having close to 20K subs on my channel comes with a price.

Still, I've managed to extract some anonymity for myself. You can Google my name and nothing will turn up. I'm Luna on IG. LoRez on TikTok. To my fans, I'm only Reiko.

I recall the first shoot I had produced with Nicole, my partner. We drove her father's Mercedes to a multi-storey carpark at this industrial estate. Had to keep an eye out for police patrols and pervs loitering around.

I had put on dark eyeliner, glass fragments irrigating my cleavage and knee-high boots draped over the door of the car. We tried out different angles and took a couple of shots. Nicole helped with the editing, while I set up the account and uploaded the content, both of us keeping our fingers crossed.

You know how things can change overnight? Let's just say when the money rolled in, we couldn't believe our eyes.

My most downloaded content: me in a nurse's uniform trapped between the steering wheel, dashboard lights brightening my face. And as a convent girl writhing about in twisted metal, petrol fumes and engine coolant, blood tickling from the corner of my mouth.

To tell you the truth, I do feel sorry for all those guys. Even if we do meet in person, they can't find the courage to say hello. For them, I exist only in pixels and gigabytes. It must really hurt, wondering what's it like to touch me and never being able to produce an answer they could understand. (300 words)

Patrick Sagaram's work has appeared in QLRS and anthologies such as *Best New Singaporean Short Stories* and *How We Live Now: Stories of Daily Living*. He lives in Singapore and works as a teacher.

Ellen's Secret

John Evan P. Orias

It was eight o'clock when I started getting ready for the big night. The anticipation was killing me as I opened my laptop, logged into my account, and began the show.

In a matter of minutes, one of the regular clients sent me a private message.

"Hi, Ellen! It's Marvin! How are you?" he wrote.

I took a deep breath and replied, "Hi, daddy! I'm good. How about you?"

"Lonely..." he responded.

"Well, I have new videos here if you like," I replied, trying to lighten the mood.

"Great! You make me feel very excited," he typed.

I could not help but feel uncomfortable talking to strangers—especially older men—about intimate topics. It's not easy to put on a persona and indulge their desires, but I had to remind myself this was just a job. I quickly uploaded the files, and within a matter of minutes, the client unlocked every video available. After he left the chat, I received more private messages from VIPs and new clients.

As payment notifications rolled in, I felt a sense of satisfaction, but something was missing. This type of work was not what I wanted to do. I dreamed of becoming a writer, but passion was not enough to feed me. This paid the bills and allowed me to live the life I wanted. I knew I had to break out of this dream loop. As the clock struck midnight, I closed my laptop and went to bed. All I had to do was respond to chats and sell videos, while Ellen was free to enjoy her everyday life. (266 words)

John Evan P. Orias is a writer and researcher. He holds a BA in Journalism and MA in Communication (cum laude) from the University of Santo Tomas, where he also won several awards for his literary works. His short stories and essays have been published in various anthologies.

Digging out the Truth
Twisstii

Twisstii is an illustrator based in Singapore. Driven by an insatiable need to doodle on any possible surface, she combines her love for fresh paper with doodling. Other than her unsuspecting cats, she counts various vintage ephemera as her inspiration.

The Proposal
Kat Chua

Sal texted her, "Let me come over. I need to see you." Never mind that he had a girlfriend, waiting, back at his apartment. Never mind that he was thirty-three, and she was just a high school student. He was her first boyfriend; she had to forgive him for these faults.

That day, he loved her so tenderly she felt as if her limbs would come off. It was an unscrewing, a dismantling into separate pieces, and then: floating. Afterwards, he whispered, "I'm going to ask Lily to marry me."

She nodded, kissed him congratulations, and hoped fervently that she wouldn't be as lost at thirty-three. (106 words)

Kat Chua is a writer and data scientist. She grew up in Singapore and received her BA from UC Berkeley. She lives in Chicago.

Nipa Hut
Euginia Tan

When all was quiet and even the cicadas' chirping dwindled into slumber, the old man watched the lad and Merlynn copulate. His lower belly and groin pulsated with the memory of lovemaking, the feeling of touch against his ribs reignited. The lad, though cold and callous in the day, became a romantic when the curtain of night fell over the nipa hut. He cooed sweet nothings to Merlynn, fondling her tired breasts and hips, kissing her strained neck. She giggled, and somehow, the act would begin.

The old man was not observant, things led from one thing to another, like how Pac-man threw punches to swift victory on television. He could no longer track them, only when they began or ended.

He watched the lad clamber on top of Merlynn, virile as a bull, persistent in his penetration. Merlynn stifled moans of pleasure, just as his own wife did in their youth, afraid to wake the baby or appear unchaste. The nipa hut shivered after they finished. The old man's breathing quickened together with the lovers, panting and receding, their chests and stomachs bobbing. Old and young moved in tandem, momentary relief from coarse living, in the nipa hut.

He passed his numbered days without a calendar. When his ears were keen, he caught the throngs of distant church bells clanging, the scatter of wheels from bicycles and jeepneys and always, the sound of more stone stacked on ground. As long as his skyline did not blight with the height of a skyscraper, he was free. He hoped that death would be kind, as he sighed on the steps of the nipa hut's doorway, the water colour of village life preserved albeit murky in the cataracts of his vision and mind. (291 words)

Euginia Tan is a multidisciplinary Singaporean writer who writes poetry and plays. She also pens curatorial essays for visual artists based in Singapore. She enjoys cross-pollinating art into multidisciplinary platforms and reviving stories. Contact her at eugtan@hotmail.com.

Love Missed
Audrey Tay

I knew from the beginning that I would never make him mine.

The sparse hairs dotting a slack jaw and tracing an uneven march to encircle a thin mouth, the flaccid body clothed in the habitual uniform of an untucked monochrome shirt over un-ironed pants, the slovenly slouching gait: The antithesis of what I could tolerate in a partner.

He was undeterred. Cognisant of his failings, he made up for them in his puppy eagerness to please. He was unstinting in his acceptance of my mercurial moods when I had to fight my demons. His was the comforting presence that gave me the force to ride out my storms.

I was drawn in, so deep I could not walk away.

But in the end, he was the one who did. Now I know he would never make me his. (139 words)

Audrey Tay stumbled into writing when as a child, she spun stories to fool her parents into thinking she was hard at schoolwork. As an adult, when not pandering to her pampered pooch, she writes short stories. Her story, "Maid in Singapore", was published in the anthology *Singapore at Home: Life Across Lines*.

Infinite Chances
Rye Antonio

Rye Antonio is a writer, artist, and occasional storyteller based in Metro Manila.

The Hum
Margaret Tang

We gather for the obligatory Sunday dinner with parents, siblings and their spouses. Nothing much changes. We still work at the same companies. Our children still school at the same schools. We keep our same routines, same hobbies, same chores. We have nothing new to tell each other. So, we lob inconsequential stories into the air to pass time.

Afterwards, we drive the same route along Upper Thomson Road. The path sways right and left and up and down over the mounds of the central catchment area. My eyes take in the same condos, same shophouses, same trees, same, same, same.

We slip in and out of the grey of night and orange glow of each passing streetlight. The rainforest trees rock their boughs and shadows in the wind. The tyres strum the asphalt while the air-conditioner hums a dull lullaby. The engine drones on until we reach that section where nature reigns and the road and the lampposts are the only signs of humans. Here, the forest looks as it did a century ago when tigers used to roam the lush undergrowth. This lung of green has exhaled oxygen and collected water for as long as Singapore can remember. Constant and unwavering, it is the nourishing soul of this island.

The sounds meld into a constant hum. Gradually, I notice the quiet breathing of the man driving. He is constant and unwavering. A comforting calm hugs me. I am not alone.

I will never be alone.

He feels my gaze upon him. "What is it?"

"I love you."

I snuggle into the warmth of my seat and rejoice over the constant rituals of my life. (276 words)

Margaret Tang is a Singaporean short story writer whose work has appeared in anthologies. She won the competition, *Diversity in Words*, in 2015. She writes as a means to explore the meaning of love, friendships and relationships.

Fish Bowl
Melissa Salva

The fish in the plastic bowl has no name. The bowl has a few pebbles but no water plants or air pump. It gets a quick rinse every week and a half. The extent of care the fish receives is a sprinkling of semi-ground pellets every day. The pinches are generous when the kids fight over who gets to feed it. Otherwise, it's largely forgotten.

The bowl sits on the kitchen table where we park the hot muffin pan, unload the groceries, peel the vegetables. I don't think twice about gutting fish there.

Every day, I peer into the bowl to check if the fish is alive. It's the last of the three fantail guppies we got for a school project a couple of months back. Does it think about the lake, or wherever it came from.

And is its tiny brain entirely devoted to just keeping its fins moving? Yesterday when I looked, it wasn't moving at all, and I was somehow relieved. I thought about what kind of statement it would make, to die in a small plastic bowl that had just a few pebbles and a confetti of fish food littering the water's surface. To die, despite having everything you need. But the fish was not dead. It was merely asleep, and it darted across the bowl when it sensed my movement.

I sat at the dining table to do something equally inconsequential, every once in a while looking up to glance at the passing sedan, the school bus, the SUV, the neighbour in her leg warmers, the yayas sunning the babies, the maids walking the dogs, the tweens on skateboards, the village gardener pruning the trees, the sun staining everything orange, my husband coming home from work, the lamppost automatically switching on. (296 words)

Melissa Salva took graduate studies in Creative Writing at the University of the Philippines Diliman. She writes contemporary fiction, children's books, and poetry.

Feline Sovereignty
Peter Loh

A self-taught illustrator and graphic designer, Peter Loh has a prolific portfolio that includes numerous local and US projects, ranging from books, explainer videos, infographics and logo designs, to live caricature drawing at corporate events. He has also conducted art lessons for schools and offices, as well as for charities and non-profit organisations.

Velvet
Carmie Ortego

"There's not much to feel here, is there?" she says as she fingers the smooth leaves of the mabolo. *I direct her to the underside of the leaf where it is a bit more furry.*

"Soft hairs. Of course." Her other hand reaches blindly for the fruit covered with fine reddish down. She palms it this time, rocking it up and down as she weighs it lightly.

This is how she tries to see, months after the doctors told us she would never regain her sight. First the callus, so she is not afraid to feel, and then the sensation, so she knows exactly what it was.

"Talk to me," she says as she cups my face and starts feeling the roundness of my cheeks, the set of my jaw.

I need to hear you, she doesn't say, so this silence would not be another darkness to bear. So I tell her about the cane I'm building for her, how I'm going to get it from the mabolo wood whose leaves and fruit she has just touched. The handle has special carvings, I add, so when she grips it, she'd know it's hers. It's just going to be a bit heavy, I warn her, and she nods. *No coddling,* we silently agree. Her strength is not lost with her sight. And all the while she hasn't stopped mapping my face, ending at my left temple, where unfortunately a pimple is budding.

"This is new," she says. "Must be the time of the month."

I whisper *yes* as I feel my face heat up. From where I am, there is no room for the rough so she doesn't stumble with her hands. From where she is, memory is clarity, and another imperfection is a new way to recognise me. (298 words)

Carmie Ortego is a native of Talalora, Samar. She graduated with a Master of Fine Arts in Creative Writing degree at De La Salle University-Manila. Her poems and essays have been published in national and international publications. Currently, she teaches at the Senior High School Department of NU MOA.

First Love
Rosie Wee

Laura yawned and opened her eyelids a little, only to be greeted by the warm morning light, which sparkled and winked at her as if it knew about the kiss. She smiled, for Kevin Song had appeared in her dream. How lovely it had all been—her blue chiffon dress with its ruffles, the whiff of Old Spice, and the kiss. Laura pulled at her duvet and strained to relive those magnetic moments, but they faded behind the curtain which hung before her closed eyelids.

"Grandma. Happy Valentine's Day! I bought roses for you," said Khai in his chirpy voice. "I waited quite a while for you to wake up. You were smiling in your sleep. Was it a sweet dream?"

Laura answered with a faint smile. With some effort, Khai propped her up with pillows. He put a soft wrap around her thin shoulders and tidied her wispy hair. The years had thinned her once lustrous hair and sprayed it with grey. Her once peach-cream complexion was stippled by a configuration of nutmeg spots.

"Well, Grandma, you need to sign the pension form so that I can deliver it to the Ministry of Education."

Laura rested her gnarled and arthritis-ridden hands on the makeshift table as Khai walked away to answer a call.

When he came back, he stared at the completed form. "Grandma, your surname is Sim, not Song. S-I-M." After some effort, she wrote the correct one.

But her eyes, brimming with tears, spoke to him. (249 words)

Rosie Wee is a retired secondary school Department Head of English and the author of a historical novel, *The Heart Remembers*. She has had two pieces, "A House Full of Memories in Saunders Road" (7 Nov 2021), and "A Room Full of Memories in an Old Mansion" (19 Dec 2021), published in *The Sunday Times*.

Monorail
Daren Shiau

At least we have this week, Din whispered, his hand grasping hers so tightly that her ring bit into his palm. Actually it's just… four days, she replied. Four days, he repeated staring at the track. The elevated train pulled slowly into the station. It was packed and smelt of suntan lotion. February is a short month Din, Noor reminded him. The twenty-eighth falls on the coming Tuesday. He dug his nails into his palm, and the only thing he could think of was the whole day ahead of them. (90 words)

Daren Shiau is an author of five books, including a seminal collection of microfiction, *Velouria* (2007), which was reprinted in 2017 with a new story, "Sedimentary", that received the top prize in *The Straits Times'* inaugural microfiction collection in 2007. He currently serves as Co-Chair of the Singapore Writers Festival advisory panel.

Girl, Gilded
Andy Lopez

After the full-body Restructuration you stand outside your lover's door. *What've you done?* you imagine her saying. Touching your ribcage (frills of sputtered steel), the flare of your shoulder (ruby-encrusted weapons of destruction), you'll tell her it doesn't hurt. Somewhere, the ocean is disassembling itself, overriding your data file with ribbons of salt and mineral. All the old hurts decay: the boy who collared a hand around your throat; the pew, where you poured yourself empty; the sweet cherub's mouth above. How you've learned from its indifferent terracotta stillness. *I'm still here*, you'll say. *Still holy.* (96 words)

Andy Lopez lives and writes in the Philippines. She has received writing fellowships from GrubStreet and the University of Santo Tomas. Her work has been published and is forthcoming in the *Best Small Fictions 2021, Split Lip Magazine*, and other publications. Contact her at andy-lopez.weebly.com.

Always
Eli Ampil Gagelonia

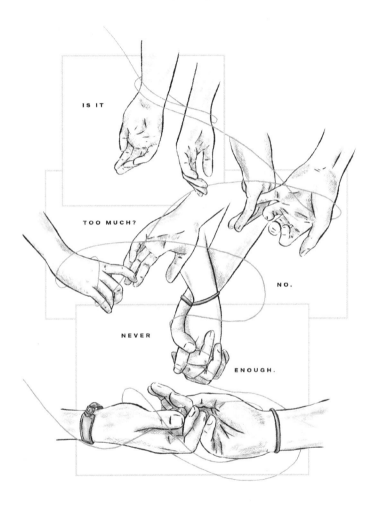

Eli Ampil Gagelonia is a Filipino creative director and multimedia designer by trade who indulges in illustration and a little bit of writing in her spare time. Her love for storytelling, whether through visuals or writing, has been a constant in her life

Missing Things
NY Chua

I don't know, John. This keeps on happening. Did you try using your eyes, for once?

There it was, Julia's tone, the exasperated one, dripping with disdain, the one John knew too well from decades of marriage.

The last time he misplaced something was just the other day. It was tickets to a play they were going to see, one of the diversions on this winter trip visiting their adult children.

After hopelessly searching through coat and pant pockets, and the messy open suitcase which didn't know whether it was staying or leaving, lying sadly on the hotel room floor, John spied one of the half-hidden zippers on his backpack. With Julia hovering over him like a vulture, he excitedly unzipped it.

The angels in heaven erupted in loud chorus, and a ray of beatific light illuminated the tiny unzipped compartment. The tickets were there. John was filled with sudden non-commensurate joy and did a disco move, his belly flouncing over his pants. Julia rolled her eyes and walked away.

That was yesterday. Today, John couldn't find his keys, and before his mind had processed it, he blurted out loud, *Julia, have you seen my keys*?

He mentally kicked himself. Now he could hear Julia's heavy footsteps coming from the living area.

John frantically grabbed his backpack and contemplated the same tiny pocket, that magic compartment that seemed to yield all that had been lost in their many years of marriage. With hope hammering in his chest, he held the zipper and prayed that the keys would be there; that all that was lost would be found, one more time. (270 words)

NY Chua is a financial adviser, and has had short fiction and poetry published in several anthologies in Singapore.

Transient
John Gilford Auxilio Doquila

He booked a flight to a city where no one knew him but his sadness. He dropped into a pub seeking solace in sorrow, thinking it would bring catharsis, and he would magically heal. Wasn't this the promise of the modern world?

His breath reeked of alcohol, and his tongue met foreign lips that spoke of the same tragedy. Pain is a universal language, but the brightest, widest smiles mask grief. He even danced with strangers, only to mock his own affliction. Why cry when you can dance?

He continued masturbating his sadness.

He went on a date, seeking fleeting refuge in a stranger. In the taxi's backseat, their knees brushed against each other. He rested his palm on his legs, and his fingers tapped his skin, music to his throbbing heart or cock. What was the difference?

In a rented room where he was promised salvation or damnation, he first kissed the stranger's shoulders like he always did with a past lover. Next, he kissed his neck and finally his lips. He looked him in the eye, wanting to be told, "I love you." Such a foolish act, but don't we all want to be loved? Even just for a night?

As if conjuring a lost love, he went on trailing his map of grief on the stranger's body. They both finished and arrived at the destination of another fleeting satisfaction, but his sorrow never left.

"See you next time," the stranger said. He nodded and smiled. He walked away from the narrow street lit in blood red by the hotel's outdated marquee and hailed a taxi.

He wished there would be no next time. (276 words)

John Gilford Auxilio Doquila is a graduate of the University of the Philippines. He holds a degree in English (Creative Writing). He is proudly queer, a hopeless romantic, and a furdad. He was born and raised in Cagayan de Oro, earned a writing degree in Davao, and continues to write stories in Quezon City.

Packages
Inez Tan

Every year around Christmas, the packages arrived. They weren't for me. They were for the people who previously lived in the flat, Roy and Alice Teo. I assumed they'd come from relatives who weren't important or liked enough to have been given their new address. But then it was unusual that they'd send gifts.

I didn't have their new address either. Neither did the real estate agent. Roy and Alice Lee didn't show up in any online searches. So I figured they must be very old. They hadn't died, though.

According to the agent, they had just gone somewhere else. Their flat had been loved, I could tell. Every detail, from the pipes to the paint, had been thought through. I couldn't have asked for better.

When all my friends started posting about their BTOs and their dream houses, I made a promise to myself: I would never care for a home that way. But the Teos' flat made me change my mind.

The mystery of the packages continued. I left the packages in the downstairs lobby where someone else could take them. They were always claimed.

My third Christmas in the flat, the packages arrived again. For the first time, one came with a card. It read: *I know Eliza would have been twelve years old this year. I remember these were her favourite.*

The package contained a glass jar of spiced pears from a company with "&" in its name, tied with a wide red ribbon. I ate the contents straight out of the jar. I still think about how those pears tasted, heavy with syrup and sorrow.

Sometimes you want people to know what you've been through. Sometimes you don't.

The whole time I lived in that flat, no mail came for me. (296 words)

Inez Tan is the author of the national bestseller *This Is Where I Won't Be Alone: Stories*. An educator and Kundiman fellow, she holds an MFA (Fiction) from the University of Michigan and an MFA (Poetry) from the University of California, Irvine. Check out her website at ineztan.com.

The Consequence of Uncontrolled Shopping in 2020

Arif Rafhan

Post-quarantine commitment

Arif Rafhan bin Othman is a comic artist, a mural artist, an animator, a doodler and a neighbourhood art teacher in both digital and analogue medium. His work has spanned from paintings, book illustrations (for MPH & Fixi), graphic novels (Marshall Cavendish, MPH & Maple Comics), graphic facilitation (BNM & PruBSN), corporate comics and art installation for corporate offices.

Maggie, Me, and the Ducati
Verena Tay

I had a dream. My girlfriend was a real hot babe, like Maggie Q. My bike was also a sizzler, a Ducati 1098. Maggie, me and the Ducati were cruising down a highway. The Ducati shot forward like a black panther. Maggie sat behind me, holding me closer, her cheek tender on my shoulder, her hair streaming in the wind. Riding with me was bringing her to heaven. I had it all.

My dream came true. Sort of.

A Ducati? Hah! As if I can afford! More like Yamaha—you know how long it took me to save up for just a simple motorbike? Anyhow, my girlfriend rode pillion last week. Well, she's not my girlfriend, just a friend who's a girl, if you know what I mean.

Meg needed to get from poly to town. I offered her a ride. Now Meg's on the plump side, but oh man! I didn't know she was going to weigh down the Yamaha so damn much that it was crawling all the way to Orchard! Even worse, it was Meg's first time on a bike. She held onto me so tight, I couldn't breathe! She screamed in my ear so loud, *I thought I'd go deaf*!

If that is what it means to have a girlfriend, fuck the dream! I don't need it all. I'll choose the Yamaha over a girl anytime. (230 words)

A Singapore-based writer, editor, storyteller, theatre practitioner and arts educator, Verena Tay (verenatay.com) has published two collections of short stories and four volumes of plays, as well as edited twelve story anthologies. She has just completed a PhD in Creative Writing with Swansea University.

Shoegaze Girl
Ian Rosales Casocot

Her name was Sophie. Life of the party. She'd tell people she met for the first time, whether they asked her or not, that her name was derived from the Greek word for "wisdom"—then pause dramatically, as if expecting applause. But she had a grand way of carrying a conversation, and for her circle, she was charming, beautiful, and capable of dispensing wisdom. "I believe that marriage is blah blah blah…" For goodness' sake, she was only 21! She had hangers-on, would you believe. But that was when she found herself pregnant by her tattoo-artist boyfriend. We heard they got married in Manila, but the rumour was it was a hysterical pregnancy. They came back to Dumaguete to be *artistes*, and we'd see both go around various cafes, working on their sketches. The husband was quiet, and clearly more talented. She drew loops that went nowhere. He was confronting death and hell in his sketches, which freaked us out and made us fans. "Your art's fantastic," we'd say. She was the one who'd reply: "Our art is about love! Family! Death!" Then she tried being a singer. She was in her ukulele phase, when she heard somebody say: "She sings like she's whispering to lilies before they die." After a black period where she kept making thick drawings in black pastel, she announced she was done with the ukulele and was now into shoegaze music. Then her husband remarked out of the blue: "That's good. That way you'll be whispering to your shoes, and lyrics won't matter." She went berserk. She climbed a table at a café we frequented, and—with her hands raised up to the cobwebbed ceiling, cried: "Art! I'm making only art!" We have not seen Sophie since. (292 words)

Ian Rosales Casocot taught literature, writing, and film at Silliman University in Dumaguete City, Philippines. Author of the fiction collections, *Don't Tell Anyone, Bamboo Girls, Heartbreak & Magic*, and *Beautiful Accidents*, his novel *Sugar Land* was longlisted for the 2008 Man Asian Literary Prize. He was Writer-in-Residence for the International Writers Program of the University of Iowa in 2010.

Wifi Password
Daryll Fay Gayatin

We were in the living room, and you told me to turn on my laptop, open the browser, and type in the link given by the internet service providers. Click the account button and sign in. Go to settings.

If I was confused, I should look at the bottom of our router and the sticker with the needed information. I had to edit the network name and remember the new password. Thirteen letters. No capitalisations or numbers.

Simple enough.

You put a finger to your lips. *Our secret*, you said. That I shouldn't tell anyone, not even our relatives visiting from afar who asked to connect. In exchange, the network's new name would be mine with the word *gwapa*. I laughed but didn't refuse— who didn't want to be called beautiful?

You said I should change it regularly. If someone found out the password, I had to change it, no matter what. That was the task you had given me.

After many months, I decided to do it. Alone in the same living room, laptop whirring on my lap. The site asked if I should apply and save the changes. I clicked the exit button instead. (196 words)

Daryll Faye Gayatin is from Isulan, Sultan Kudarat. She's taking up BA English (Creative Writing) at the University of the Philippines Mindanao.

Window
Clement Wee

Every evening, I walk up to the window and look out across the street.

My eyes trail up from the cars on the road to the tall residential block. I count the floors, first from ground up, then from skylight down, to make sure I have got the correct floor. Then I sweep my gaze across the units and observe which are lit, which are dim, which have clothing hung on balconies, and which have blinds pulled down.

But every evening, the row is empty. If it is windy, perhaps some laundry may flap in the wind. Perhaps I imagine a scene from a Hollywood movie where two protagonists wave at each other from opposite sides of the street. But the road is a deep canal separating Hell from the Bosom of Abraham.

As I continue surveying the row of units, lined up like matchboxes, my heart begins to ache. The stillness of the air just worsens the ache. I think of dreams I once had, hopes and visions for the future.

I blink back a couple of tears moistening the corner of my eyes.

When the sky darkens, I plop down on the sofa and wonder about the only thing left to wonder: will she return the marriage bed I bought? (212 words)

Clement Wee is a member of the Rainforest Writers' Group affiliated to SingLit Station. He has been interested in stories ever since he read *The NeverEnding Story* as a child. He enjoys stories with complex worlds and deep emotions, and aspires to create his own sci-fi world someday.

Woke
Felix Cheong and Clio Ding

Felix Cheong is the author of 25 books across different genres, from poetry to graphic novels. His works have been widely anthologised and nominated for the prestigious Frank O'Connor Award and the Singapore Literature Prize. Conferred the Young Artist Award in 2000, Felix has been invited to writers festivals all over the world, such as Edinburgh, Austin, Sydney and Christchurch.

Clio Ding is an art educator and comic artist who is obsessed with fishes and cheeses. She also writes about Singapore comics for SG Cartoon Resource Hub.

How We End
Amy Chia

You hung garlands around her neck. A confession, that's how you met. The plastic you swiped to pay those fifty bucks. A supplementary of *my* Mastercard. Another five hundred goes that extra mile. All two inches of you in her land of smiles. Then you fooled her by flaunting my money. She believed you and wanted to marry.

When the bills came, you lied away. Stuff for Mother, you quickly said. Your *Mother* called me at 3am. In half English, she purred you're her man. How dare you blame, it was all my fault. I'm always working, we often fought. On shaking knees, you solemnly vowed, from that day on, to never leave the house. But I changed the lock and cancelled your cards. Better alone than keep a fool and his tart. (133 words)

Amy Chia is a freelance copywriter and marketing consultant, who is currently pursuing an MA Creative Writing. Her prose has been published in an anthology *Letter to My Partner*. She is working on a collection of travel flash fiction.

Space Oddity
Jocelyn Low

Daniel and I practised break-ups with varying degrees of seriousness over the four years we were together. One time we split for three months. He went to Nepal and got high every night.

"How could you go to Nepal without me?"

"But we were over, baby. I thought it was for real."

"Daniel…" I traced the small ankh tattooed below his right ear, a twin to the one on my left ankle.

"Without you in my life, I'll be like Major Tom floating around in my tin can. You're my ground control, okay?"

"Stop passing off Bowie's lyrics as your own, la!" Daniel hugged me tighter and kissed my forehead.

Now when I see Daniel at public events, we pretend we don't know each other. But I find that I don't know what to do with my face, or hands. The only thing I can think of is to pay closer attention to Wei. I met Wei nine months after Daniel and I broke up. (*For the last time,* we told ourselves.) Standing close to the stage with the other fans, I wrap my body around Wei's, and kiss him openly. I try to make him open his mouth, so I can feel his tongue, but he's too shy. He kisses me back—his lips soft, apologetic. He is not used to such public displays of affection.

"Clarice." I almost cannot hear him above the music.

"What?"

I laugh into his open face, desperate to quell my rising panic. I worry that Daniel can see me doing this with Wei. I worry that Daniel cannot see me doing this with Wei. Then I wonder if Daniel will be in time to catch me, as I float higher and higher into the dark sky. (293 words)

Jocelyn Low reads so much that she sometimes dreams in text form, with proper punctuation and paragraphing. She enjoys writing as it allows her to be many selves living many lives. Jocelyn loves teaching and cats. Her work has appeared in *Anak Sastra* and LASALLE College of the Arts' anthology *SAMPAN*.

Big Day
Chan Ziqian

When Mat and I took the train to go sign the divorce papers, we held hands all the way. Outside the lawyer's office, he said, "Maybe we shouldn't," he nodded at our clasped hands, "in case they don't let us get a divorce." The receptionist thought we were there for a property purchase and showed us to a room with a landscape painting. When she realised her mistake, she ushered us a few doors down where ugly abstract art—slashes of red and black—hung on the wall.

Afterwards, Mat and I went for dinner near City Hall. We sat on a rattan sofa outside the restaurant in the warm evening light. I had a cocktail with blackberries and a cinnamon stick floating in it. He had cubes of tuna decorated with edible flowers. We didn't often eat at places like this. The last time was our wedding reception ten years ago. Back then we had been nervous, surrounded by our extended families, and had forgotten to take any photos. With no one around this time, we made faces and posed for wefies.

I still have these photos. Every year on this date, my phone reminds me of them. In them, our heads are close together, filling the frame. What you don't see is how our bodies are lightly touching at the shoulders and knees. It's been four years, and I still know how his arm feels against mine. When I take a deep breath, I can smell his underarm odour, a combination of dill and curry. People assume you get divorced because you can't stand each other. I want to tell them, you know, after signing the papers, we held hands all the way to dinner too. (288 words)

Chan Ziqian works as an editor. Her short stories have appeared in *QLRS* and *Ceriph*, among others.

Living in the Moment
Alan Bay

Alan Bay is a comic artist and illustrator who enjoys spreading happiness through his drawings. He likes to keep the spirit of childhood alive by drawing big monsters, magical dragons and pesky kids.

And Then

Noelle Q. de Jesus

Never once was he not in mind, more than he'd ever been when he was alive, no matter where she was or what she was doing. She heard his voice from beyond. Confiding, sometimes, commanding, yet other times full of regret and familiar longing, even though in these last years of ugly illness, there had been no time for romance.

Not even a year after, she found herself in the city for work, which was where they'd met lifetimes ago. They savored the strangeness of fruit tossed in sweet black sauce and chili. They laughed at the giant, scaly-tailed, maned creature of stone, as they wandered along the river, relishing the thrill of starting to know each other. Somehow she forgot all this (how could she ever forget?), until day's end. As she walked that same river back to the hotel beneath a sky that blushed pink, she was at once so overcome by the weight of her heart, tears spilled from her eyes into noodles she could not eat.

Again, just as it happened every night of this horrible year, she sat up in bed unable to sleep, her eyes open because the pain of seeing him when they were closed was too much to bear. Now she heard his voice distinctly, "I know it's hard, but you can do it." Wondering what it was she was supposed to do, she glanced out the window and saw him sitting by a window across, seated at a table, head bent in the gleam of a laptop. When he looked up, the face she saw fixed on hers wasn't his at all. It was her own. (275 words)

Noelle Q. de Jesus is author of two short fiction collections: *Cursed and Other Stories* (Penguin Random House SEA 2019) and *Blood Collected Stories* (Ethos Books Singapore 2015), the 2016 Next Generation Indie Book Awardee for the Short Story. She was editor of the *Fast Food Fiction* collections (2003, 2015). She has a novel in progress, but microfiction remains a distraction.

The Ghost Marriage
Dave Chua

Ying is surprised that instead of Daniel, the guy she is supposed to meet from the dating app, she is approached by a grey-haired couple. They explain that they are the ones who have been using the app, accessing it using the password from their son's digital will.

"He died several months ago," the mother explains. Ying does not know what to say, so she lets them talk, wondering how she can extricate herself without seeming cruel.

The older man explains. "We would like you to marry our son. In the afterlife."

He knows the practice is no longer done, but they cannot stand the thought of their son sitting under a table, picking up scraps dropped from the plates of the married. "That is the fate of the unmarried in the afterlife," the mother laments. It seems that even in the afterlife, singles are discriminated against

They want to make it "financially viable", which does get Ying's attention. They will ensure that the flat they own goes to her.

The ceremony is performed in their cavernous flat. Ying stands next to a papier-mâche model of Daniel dressed in a black suit while a medium chants.

After the ceremony, she moves in. Her new in-laws summon up photos and after the third week, their stories repeat themselves, but the joy in their faces makes Ying relish the happiness she can bring to them. They say that he brought back a starving calico kitten and played bass guitar at a company concert and how they are sure Ying would have been proud of him and his kindness.

As she sleeps on his bed, she sometimes imagines, but never dreams, of his spectral hand on her chest. Weightless, yet the heaviest thing in the world. (293 words)

Dave Chua's first novel, *Gone Case*, received a Singapore Literature Prize Commendation Award in 1996, and was adapted into a graphic novel and mini-series. His collection, *The Beating and Other Stories*, was longlisted for the 2012 Frank O'Connor International Short Story prize. He has also written TV scripts, including HBO's *Invisible Stories*.

Playback
Yeo Wei Wei

The day after E died, I received texts from him. They arrived and disappeared, leaving no proof of having existed. Until the day his body was cremated, I texted him to explain my decision to leave him and left messages on his voicemail. When I told my best friend, she made an appointment for me to see a grief counsellor. Each time, I sat in my work clothes across from the counsellor, a retired air force pilot. My weeping was spread out over ten sessions. E had a lot of possessions, so I had a lot to process. He owned an iMac, a MacBook Pro, an iPad and a Kindle. I learnt new things about him. Things I hadn't understood before began to make sense. By then, I'd stopped texting him. Instead, I talked to him as I cleaned our flat or as I lay on our bed, hugging his pillow. There were hundreds of photos of E and his exes on his computers. He'd mentioned this before, how many women he'd dated before he met me. I studied the photos and listened to his playlists named after people—Mum, Chloe, Jacqui, Sandra and so on. There wasn't one for me because we were still together when he died. The last time we spoke, I'd told him it was over but he said no, it wasn't. More than ten years after E's death, I thought of his Instagram and searched for it. There were posts from the day he died to the present; no captions. One of them showed a spotted dove nestling beside my Calliandra plant. I recognised the bird immediately. It was a nuisance, forever cooing. Doves mate for life. That day, I blocked E from following me and removed myself from his followers. (296 words)

Yeo Wei Wei's fiction and translations have appeared in anthologies and journals, including the *Best New Singaporean Short Stories* anthology, *Brooklyn Rail*, *Mascara Literary Review*, and *QLRS*. In 2023, two collections of translations, transcreations and adaptations of Chinese short stories, *Diasporic* and *Clan*, were published in Singapore, UK and US.

Love and its New Forms
Sara Florian

"...Dear Soul,

what was I telling you? Ah, yes, when you are a child it'd be useful to get a manual of instructions for your adult life, methinks, especially in preparation for times of emotional turmoil. Is love a sea whirlwind one gets lost into or a smooth-sailing lake? Do feelings run along a river of universal truths or are we tied to the mechani(ci)sm of metropolises, enveloped by blankets of people all the time? Yet, as loneliness is not just a state of mind, it is really hard to connect with people...like, we all have social medias, but the idea of being connected, no, I mean, the "essence" of relationships, how has that cocooned in a virtual –metaphysical– nest in such a short time span?"

Is true, deep love still possible at the edge of a post-pandemic, dystopian, cosmopolitan {life-full-of-loneliness} and of [virtual alienation]? What spurs the heartbeats taking the **HELM** of our capacity to love towards blooming into new forms of expression? How do our *souls* evolve in the unravelling of facts, both real and virtual, through the *aeons* of time?

Sara Florian loves writing, painting and travel. After a PhD in Italy, she obtained a Postdoctoral Visiting Fellowship at Singapore Management University. Her work has been featured at the Poetry Festival Singapore in 2019, 2020, and 2021, at the St. Martin Book Fair (Caribbean) and at the 2022 Medellín International Poetry Festival (Colombia). Website: https://s4r4fl0ri4n.wixsite.com/my-site

An Affair
Angelo R. Lacuesta

He realised his wife had been having an affair when he found that the cable TV connection in their bedroom suddenly worked. A few days later, that stubborn bathroom light switch started working smoothly again, just like that. He decided to wait for the leaky toilet, the sticky doorframe, that burnt-out fuse to fix themselves before he would stop forgiving her. (159 words)

Angelo R. Lacuesta has written twelve books and a number of films. He is editor-at-large at *Esquire Philippines* and President of PEN (Poets, Essayists, Novelists) Philippines. His most recent book is the novel *Joy*, published by Penguin Random House SEA in 2022.

Afterword

Felix Cheong
Co-Editor

Going through so many submissions was like stumbling into more than 200 blind dates all at once. After the polite introductions, he had to sift through the chaos of what worked, what didn't. The chemistry in the piece that created a combustion in his head.

Sometimes, it was a turn of phrase—how elegant the language!—that drew him in, like warming his hands over a fire. Other times, it was a turn in the plot, a sizzle and singe he didn't see coming, that did the trick.

It was the same with the graphic fiction contributions. Beyond the glow of the artwork, did it have anything interesting to say about love, family, work, art, death and everything else in-between? Did it tell a good campfire story, short and sweet?

But it wasn't the end even when the pieces came together—they had to be sorted into a thematic thread running a clear line through the book. Thankfully, he discovered that writers and artists tend to create around similar themes—family differences and indifferences, love gone awful or awry, death as the final nail, art as a redeeming force.

Of course, there were also pieces that slipped between the cracks—those he slipped in like bookstands to prop up the rest.

Like his co-editor, he was elated by the submissions pouring in from so many countries—from India to Hong Kong, from Malaysia to the Philippines, from Australia to Singapore. My, microfiction narrative is really going places!

It showed him, once and for all, that art may be long, but life—and our attention span—is shorter than we care to admit.

We hope you have enjoyed our anthology, and perhaps it has given you that nudge to pen or draw your own microfiction stories. (295 words)

Acknowledgements

The editors would like to acknowledge the work of editors and literary anthologists who came before us, that is, James Thomas, Robert Shapard, and Jerome Stern and their books, *Sudden Fiction* and *Flash Fiction*, and *Microfiction*, respectively, which introduced us to the form, and led us to its Asian counterparts and equivalents.